TAINTED

BOOK THREE IN THE *TORN* SERIES

NEW YORK TIMES AND *USA TODAY* BESTSELLING AUTHOR
K.A. ROBINSON

OTHER BOOKS BY

NEW YORK TIMES AND *USA TODAY* BESTSELLING AUTHOR

K.A. ROBINSON

THE TORN SERIES

TORN

TWISTED

TAINTED

THE TIES SERIES

SHATTERED TIES

Tainted

K.A. Robinson

Copyright © 2013 by K.A. Robinson

All rights reserved.

Cover Photo by Photographer: Hilda Yulfo

Cover Designer: Letitia Hasser, Romantic Book Designs

Cover Model: Kevin Cooley of Maggie Inc., Modeling Agency, Boston, MA

Editor and Interior Designer: Jovana Shirley, Unforeseen Editing

K.A. Robinson

Visit my Facebook page at www.facebook.com/KARobinson13

ISBN-13: 978-1494286088

ISBN-10: 1494286084

DEDICATION

This book is dedicated to those of you who followed the series and wanted more. I couldn't ask for better readers. Thank you so much for your support.

CONTENTS

A NOTE TO READERS

Tainted is broken down into three parts. "Part One: Facing My Demons" is from Drake's point of view and occurs during the six months when Chloe and Drake are apart in Twisted. "Part Two: Learning to Love Again" is from Chloe's point of view and starts three months after the end of Twisted prior to the "Epilogue" in Twisted. "Part Three: New Beginnings" is from Drake's point of view and takes place nine months after the "Epilogue" in Twisted.

Enjoy!

PART ONE

Facing My Demons
Drake

Chapter

"Wake up, asshole!" someone shouted at me.

I was too hungover to care. I groaned as I rolled over, but I refused to open my eyes. Whoever it was could go take a flying leap.

"Wake! Up!" the person yelled into my ear.

I felt like lightning was shooting through my head. My eyes opened slowly, and I saw Chloe glaring down at me. "Chloe?"

"Good job. You know who I am. Now, get up."

I instantly went on alert at the anger in her voice. She was obviously still pissed about my little scene at the bar last night.

I slowly sat up and looked at her. "Not so loud. My head is killing me."

"It's really going to hurt after I get through with you," she said as she threw something at me. "Look what fell out of your pocket."

My eyes widened as I realized what it was. I glanced back and forth between the bag and her, trying to think of something to say. "That's not mine."

"Don't lie to me, Drake. I'm not stupid! It fell out of your pocket!" she screeched.

Eric stood up from his bed and put his hand on her shoulder to keep her from attacking me. "Hey, calm down."

I watched as she turned to glare at him.

"Stay out of this. Actually, I want you guys to give us a minute alone."

"I, uh…you're kind of mad right now. I don't think that's such a good idea," Eric said.

"No, I want to be alone with him. Please."

Eric seemed unsure, but Jade nodded.

"We'll be outside. Just yell if you need us," Jade said.

Chloe waited until Eric, Jade, and Adam left to turn back to me. Neither of us spoke as we stared at each other. Her eyes welled up with tears, and I felt my chest tighten as I watched them slide down her cheeks. I knew I was causing her pain, but I didn't know how to stop it.

"How could you?" she whispered.

"I didn't—" I started.

She held up her hand. "No, just stop. Tell me the truth."

I stood and reached out for her, but she pushed me away. That hurt more than I wanted to admit. I never wanted Chloe to push me away. "Chloe, I'm sorry. I didn't mean for it to happen."

"That's a lie. If you didn't want it to happen, you wouldn't have started using to begin with. You've gone years without using. I thought you were done with this shit."

"I was. I mean, I am. Everything got to me, and I wanted a release. I never meant to keep using, but things just kept getting worse," I said, trying to explain my reasoning. I knew using made me weak, but I couldn't help it.

2

"Drugs are not a release. They're a prison. How long?"

I looked away. I was ashamed and terrified to admit just how long I'd been using cocaine again. I knew she would be disappointed, and I didn't want her to hate me any more than she already did.

"How long have you been using again?" she repeated the question.

When I looked up at her, I saw that she was actually shaking. Whether it was from pain or anger, I wasn't sure. "Since the night Kadi showed up with the pictures."

"Jesus, Drake!"

"It's not a big deal, all right?" I said defensively. If she understood that I had it under control, maybe she wouldn't be so mad.

"Not a big deal? Are you kidding me? You know what I went through with my mother, and I'm not about to go through it again with you!"

Rage filled me at the comparison to her mother. "I'm nothing like her. I would never hurt you like that!"

"You already did, Drake. You've been lying to me this entire time. And don't even get me started on your anger issues. I won't do it again. I want you to get help."

"What do you mean, help? I don't see what the big deal is, Chloe. I've got it under control."

"No, you don't, or you wouldn't still be using. I want you to go to rehab again. Please…for us."

"I'm not going to rehab, Chloe! You're overreacting to all of this!" I shouted, finally losing my temper. There was no way I was going back to rehab. Besides, I had it under control.

"Then, stop using right now!" she shouted back.

"I will when we go back home. I promise!"

"Bullshit, Drake. You can't stop. Either you go to rehab, or we're done!"

My mouth opened and closed, but no words came out.

"I mean it, Drake. Either you get your shit together, or I'm walking out the door right now, and I won't be back."

"You don't mean that, Chloe. You wouldn't just leave me like that. You love me."

"You're right. I do love you. But I have to do what's right for me, too. I can't be with you if you won't stop, Drake. I'm sorry, but I can't do that again."

"Just wait until we finish the tour, and I'll go. I swear to you, I will." I started to panic. She couldn't give up on me that easily.

"No, I won't wait that long. Either you go now, or it's over."

"Damn it! Damn it! Damn it!" I kicked the bag next to me, and the contents scattered. "Why are you doing this to me?"

"Because I love you, and I want you to get help! You haven't been on them long, and it won't be hard to stop."

"I can't do rehab. Just let me do this on my own. Please." I didn't need help. I knew I could handle this on by myself.

She shook her head. "I'm sorry, Drake, but if you won't go, then it's time for me to leave."

"You wouldn't really leave me, Chloe. Think about it. I love you. Hell, I want to marry you someday!"

I winced as I watched her face pinch up in pain. It wasn't the best time to throw that at her, but I was desperate. I loved her more than life itself, and I didn't want to lose her. Maybe if she knew just how much I loved her, she wouldn't do this to me, to us.

"Good-bye, Drake. I love you." She stepped closer to me and kissed my cheek.

"Chloe, please don't go," I pleaded.

She ignored me as she walked off the bus.

I stood there, frozen for a moment. I wasn't sure what to do. I wanted to run after her, but what good would it do? She had made up her mind about me, and nothing I said would change her decision. I kicked my bunk before running to the window. As I looked out, I saw Jade, Eric, and Adam standing next to the door, talking to Chloe. I watched as Jade held her arms out, and Chloe fell into them. My heart broke when I saw Chloe sobbing while Jade rubbed her back. When Chloe pulled away from Jade, Eric stepped up to her and hugged her tightly. I felt rage fill me as I watched another man comfort her. She was mine, yet I was the one causing her pain. It shouldn't be Eric holding her, it should've been me. How could things have gotten so fucked-up so quickly?

She stepped away from Eric and started toward her car, but Adam stopped her. He surprised me when he wrapped his arms

5

around her. Adam was never one to get all emotional, yet there he was, taking care of her. I really had fucked up.

I watched as he whispered in her ear, and she laughed. She stepped away and waved at everyone before she got into her car. She pulled away without a backward glance. I stood, frozen, as the band stood by the bus and watched her leave until she disappeared around the corner.

It seemed like hours before anyone moved again. I continued to stand by the window, unable to make myself move, as I realized that she was really gone. It wasn't just her blowing hot air in hopes of making me do what she had told me. My legs buckled, and I sank down to the floor, trying to process what had just happened.

Chloe had caught me, and now, she was gone. I looked down and realized that I was still clutching the bag that she had thrown at me. I felt rage take over as I threw it across the bus. It bounced off the table and landed on the floor a few feet away from me. One fucking bag had just ripped my life apart.

I sat there until the bus door opened, and the band walked in. I didn't bother to glance up as I saw three sets of shoes stop in front of me. I knew exactly what they were going to say, and even though I knew I deserved it, I didn't want to hear it.

"I hope it was worth it, Drake," Jade snapped.

I knew it was bad when Jade was the one to jump on me first. We were all a family, but she always tried to keep her opinions to herself.

6

"Don't, Jade. I know I fucked up. I don't need to hear it from you."

"Obviously, you do. You just let the best thing that ever happened to you walk away. How stupid are you? Are the drugs really worth losing her?" she asked.

"You know the answer to that! Of course they aren't worth losing Chloe, but what do you expect me to do? She wants me to quit the tour and go into rehab. We can't afford to cancel the rest of our shows, and I don't need rehab to stop. I can handle this on my own!"

"Fuck the band, and fuck the drugs! This is your life, Drake, and you're letting it walk away without even trying to save it."

"Just stop!" I stood and glared at her. I stepped forward until we were mere inches apart. "It's done, and there's nothing I can do to change it!"

"Back the fuck off of Jade, Drake. It's not her fault that you're a fucking idiot," Adam said as he pushed me back.

I snapped when he touched me. I drew my arm back and threw a punch that held every emotion I was feeling—pain, anger, regret, and most of all, loss. When my fist connected with his nose, he stumbled back.

"What the fuck?" he roared as his hands went to his face.

My eyes widened as I watched the blood pour from his nose. "Oh shit, I'm sorry! I didn't mean to."

"Fuck you, asshole!" He threw a punch of his own.

7

I stumbled back with the impact. My nose instantly started bleeding, and I couldn't help but laugh at the ridiculousness of the entire situation.

"What the fuck is so funny?" Adam asked.

My laughter turned to full-out howls at his words. "We're punching each other and bleeding all over the place."

The three of them stared at me like I'd lost my mind, and I had to admit that I was thinking the same thing.

I managed to stop laughing long enough to speak again. "I'm sorry, all right? I didn't mean to hit you, Adam. And I'm sorry for what happened with Chloe, but I don't know what to do to fix it. I can't go to rehab right now."

"Why not?" Eric asked.

He had been silent through all of this, and I was surprised that it was him who spoke up.

"Because we need to finish this tour. After we're done, I'll go after her. Hell, maybe she will cave and come back to me." I didn't see the latter happening, but I could hope.

Chloe was a hard-ass, but I knew she loved me. I wasn't being conceited about it. It was just something I could see. I knew the chances of her coming back were slim, but that hope would keep me going until I could stop using and find her.

And I swore to myself that I would stop using. As soon as we finished our shows, I would stop, and then she'd see just how wrong she had been by trying to force me into rehab. I'd hated it the first time, and I wasn't about to go back. I was in control this time around, and I'd be damned if I let anyone, even Chloe, try to tell me different. I knew her heart was in the right place, but she had freaked-out for nothing.

"You're insane, Drake. Chloe isn't going to come back to you, especially if you don't stop using. She's a smart girl, and she knows that she needs to protect herself," Eric said as he watched me closely.

"She doesn't need protection from me. I would never purposely hurt her. You guys have to know that."

"You've already hurt her, and you've broken her trust. You can't just go back from something like that. If you have this under control, I want you to stop using right now. Finish the tour sober, and then find her. We'll back you up if she doesn't believe you. I love you both, and I don't want to see either one of you hurting," Jade said.

I walked around her and grabbed a few napkins off the table to wipe away my blood. "I'll stop. I promise. Let's get through these last few shows, and I'll stop."

"You're seriously going to keep using even though we all know?" Eric asked incredulously.

"Chloe just walked out on me. Would you rather I found another way to deal with it?" I asked, hoping he would understand.

Jade's eyes widened. "You wouldn't cheat on her, Drake. I know you better than that."

"Chloe, drugs, and women are the only things I know. I can't go without having at least one of them."

Jade threw her hands up in the air. "You're a sick fuck, Drake Allen. Enjoy your drugs and women because you just lost everything else that was important to you, including me." She turned to stomp off the bus.

I watched as she walked down the stairs and slammed the door behind her. Great. Now, I'd not only pissed Chloe off but Jade as well. How many times could I fuck up in less than an hour? I looked up to see Adam and Eric watching me. "What?"

Adam shook his head. "I hope you get your shit together soon because I'm not going to sit here and watch you crash and burn." He turned and followed Jade down the steps.

And now, I could add Adam to the hate train, too. I glanced at Eric. Maybe he didn't hate my guts. "We cool?"

He shook his head. "We're the furthest thing from cool you could ever possibly imagine. I don't even know what to say to you. I knew something was going on with you, but I hoped that it wasn't this."

"I'm fine, Eric. Honest. Just give me some time to get my shit together, and everything will go back to normal. I'm not going to lose Chloe…at least not for forever."

"You're an idiot if you think that you haven't already lost her. I saw her face, Drake. There's no coming back from that."

"She'll be fine. Like I said, when we finish this tour, I'll stop using, and I'll find her. She loves me too much to let it all go."

I was sure of it, but Eric looked far from convinced.

"You took everything bad about her childhood and threw it back at her. You know what she had to deal with, and it's like you don't care. I can't even begin to understand your thought process right now."

"Let me handle it, okay? Just focus on our band, and I'll take care of my personal life." I was starting to get pissed off again, and on top of that, my head was still killing me. I needed to escape before I did something stupid, like hit a band member in the face. Wait, I'd already accomplished that feat.

"It's your life to live, and I'm not going to sit here and preach to you about it. I just hope you get your life together soon. If you keep it up, you're going to be out of the band, too."

His words shocked me. Never once had any of them mentioned kicking me out of the band. Sure, I knew I had been a dick lately, but I didn't see how they could want to kick me out. I was the main attraction, and they'd tank without me.

"Whatever you say, but we both know you can't get rid of me without the whole band going under."

"We'll survive. I don't want to kick you out, but we can't keep dealing with your shit."

I ignored him as I reached down and picked up the cocaine bag from where it had landed earlier. I didn't need this shit from any of them. I walked to the bathroom and slammed the door behind me before I pulled out my mirror. Fuck them all. I had this under control.

Chapter 2

She never came back, and she never called, not even once. With each passing day, the reality of my situation sank in. I'd lost her. With that reality closing in on me from all sides, I started using more. Her leaving had the opposite effect of what she'd hoped for. Her absence was pushing me to use more.

I knew I was being a dick to everyone around me, but I didn't care. The darkness surrounding me seeped into everything and everyone around me until the entire band was as down as I was. I made sure that I was ready for every show we had, so I could at least say I didn't suck at that part of my life.

When days changed to weeks, I realized that she was really gone, and my cocaine use tripled. Knowing that I'd lost Chloe sent me spiraling further and further into the darkness now consuming me. Every day, it grew worse as I realized she wasn't going to change her mind and come back. Without her, I found it hard to go on. I couldn't believe that I'd let some chick get to me like this, but she wasn't just any chick. She was my Chloe.

We had just finished our last show when Eric got the phone call that changed everything. I was sitting at the table, eating cereal and moping, while Jade and Adam were playing cards next to me. Eric came running into the bus with a huge grin on his face. He started fist-pumping while doing the most ridiculous dance.

"Dude, you look like you have a vagina," Adam said as he watched Eric with disgust.

At his words, I snorted and started choking as milk shot out of my nose and back into my bowl of cereal. I shoved it away, disappointed that my dinner had been ruined.

They all started laughing at the look of disgust on my face.

Jade patted me on the shoulder. "Nice."

"What's up?" Adam asked Eric.

"You aren't going to believe this! You remember those demo tapes we sent out to labels before we left? Well, one of them just called me. They want us to fly out to Los Angeles and record some of our new stuff for them."

Jade started screaming as Adam high-fived Eric.

"That is unbelievable! When are we supposed to be there?" Jade asked.

"They want us there two days from now. They're going to send a private plane and everything."

"Holy shit," I muttered.

I couldn't believe this was happening to us. We'd been together for years without catching any major attention.

"Let's not get our hopes up just yet, okay? They're not offering us a deal. They just want us to come out and record," Eric said.

"But they're obviously interested, right? Otherwise, they wouldn't have even bothered to contact us," Jade said as she bounced up and down in her chair.

Eric couldn't keep the smile off his face. "From what the guy said, they're definitely interested."

"Yes!" Adam said as he picked up Jade and swung her around.

I laughed. I was happy to see them excited for once. They needed this. I needed this.

"So, I take it we're going home today?" I asked.

"Yeah, we're finished with the tour now. We can go home, return the bus, and then fly out," Eric said.

My stomach flipped as I thought about flying. I wasn't afraid of flying, but I wasn't fond of it either. "Can we just drive?"

Jade looked at me like I'd lost my mind. "Drive?"

"It's been a while since I've been on a plane, and it's not something I want to do again anytime soon."

Adam grinned. "Better get used to it, pretty boy. If this takes off, we're going to be flying a lot."

"Joy," I mumbled as I laid my head on the table.

After throwing all of my stuff into my bag, I lay down in my bunk, planning to sleep the rest of the way home. We'd played three shows straight in a row over the last few days, and my body was exhausted. It seemed like I had just closed my eyes when someone started shaking me.

"You're home, asshat. Get up," Jade said.

I sat up and rubbed my eyes. I felt like complete shit. I grabbed my bag from beside my bunk and started walking to the front of the bus. Through the window, I caught sight of my house, and my heart lightened a little bit. It felt good to be home even if it was going to be only for a day.

Adam and Eric helped me grab my guitars and anything else I had stashed under the bus, and then they carried them to my door for me.

Jade followed behind us, watching me closely. "You going to be okay by yourself?"

I rolled my eyes as I unlocked the door. "Yes, mom. I'll be fine."

"Don't be a smart-ass. You know, we're all worried sick about you, Drake, and being here without...*her* will be hard on you."

"You can say her name, Jade. I won't break." I turned to look at her. "Chloe. See? I'm still standing here in one piece," I said sarcastically.

The truth was I felt broken. I was glad to be home, but I wasn't sure how I'd feel walking back into my house and seeing her things—if they were even still here.

"You know what? Fuck off, Drake. I'm trying to be understanding here, and as usual, you're being an ass." She sighed, clearly frustrated with me. "Try not to overdose before we leave for L.A." She turned and went back to the bus.

16

"Ouch," I said, pretending to be hurt.

I tried not to be bothered by the fact that I'd just pissed Jade off. She'd been temperamental since Chloe left, but now, she was downright livid. I sighed as I turned back to the door and swung it open.

"She's right, you know. This Drake sucks big, fat monkey ass. You've been acting like a big ass prick, and it stinks. I wish you'd get your shit under control before we all drown," Adam said, glaring at me.

"I'm fine. Thanks for the concern," I said.

"Bullshit. We know you're still using, and we'd be blind not to know that it's getting worse. I've sat by and said nothing, but this shit needs to end. You need help."

"Shut the fuck up! I said that I was fine. What I do is my business and no one else's!" I yelled.

"You're our friend, our brother. Of course it's our business, especially with this possible deal in L.A. We don't want to lose it because of your problem," Eric said.

I was so sick of everyone ganging up on me. It was like the whole world was plotting against me. I knew I was getting in deeper than I had originally intended, but I didn't care. What did it matter now anyway? Chloe was gone, and she wasn't going to come back.

"We just want the old Drake back," Adam added.

"Look, I'm sorry. I don't mean to be a dick. It just comes naturally. I'll try to keep my cool, okay?"

17

"We want you to get help, Drake. We don't want to lose you," Eric said with concern in his voice.

"Just drop it. I can't deal with this right now. Besides," I said, holding up my bag, "I have laundry to do."

Adam rolled his eyes. "Whatever. Deny it all you want, but you'll have to face this sometime. I just hope it's not too late when you do."

I threw my bag inside and then grabbed the things they had set down by my door. After I put those inside, I picked up my guitars. "Thanks for the concern."

With that, I walked into my house and then slammed the door in their faces. I couldn't deal with this shit right now. I slipped off my shoes and went into the kitchen, hoping that I had some food that was still edible after being gone for so long. I found a can of peaches and ate them straight from the can as I leaned against the counter.

I glanced down and froze. There was a key sitting there. I set the can down and picked up the key. I turned it over and over in my hands, thinking of Chloe. She had been here. I threw down the key and ran back to the entryway. Her shoes and spare jacket were both gone. I checked the living room next and saw that her books were gone from where she'd left them on the table. I went to the bathroom and found the same thing. Her toiletries were no longer there.

Taking a deep breath, I walked down the stairs to the basement where most of her stuff was boxed up. We'd planned on unpacking it all when we got back home. Everything was missing. I slid down the wall until I was sitting on the floor with my head on my knees. Everything was gone. She was gone. I'd hoped that her things would still be here. That maybe, just maybe, she hadn't completely given up on us. But knowing that she's come to pick up all of her shit was like being slapped across the face.

I stood and grabbed the first thing I saw—one of my uncle's stupid bowling trophies. I threw it against the wall and watched as it shattered from the force of the impact. I couldn't handle this. I was done. If she didn't want me, then fuck it. Fuck everything. Fuck *her*.

I stomped back up the stairs and grabbed the cocaine I had stashed in my bag. I walked to the couch and sat down. I poured what was left in the bag onto the glass top of my coffee table. I pulled out a credit card from my wallet and used it to crush the powder and separate it into lines.

After grabbing and rolling a bill, I snorted each line. It was more coke than I usually did at once and I felt the effects start to take over quickly. I relaxed as I lay down on the couch and stared at the ceiling. I wanted the drug to take away all my pain, my anger, and the betrayal I felt. I was so tired of feeling all the time.

Sometime later, I heard a knock on the door. I had been playing my guitar on the couch, but stopped as I stood up to see who it was. I could still feel the effects of the cocaine in my system as I stumbled to the door. The knock came again just as I reached for the knob and opened the door. Jade was standing on the porch, holding a bag of food from the Mexican restaurant by her house. My stomach growled loudly as I smelled the food. I hadn't realized just how hungry I was until then.

She looked concerned as she took in my appearance. "You okay?"

Between the coke and finding out that Chloe had moved all of her things out, I knew I had to look like shit. "I'm fine. I was just messing around with my guitar."

"Oh, okay then." She held up the bag. "I come bearing food. Consider it a peace offering."

I swung open the door to let her pass by me. I followed as she walked past the living room and straight into the kitchen. After setting the bag on the counter, she pulled out two to-go boxes and handed one to me while stashing the other one in my refrigerator. I grabbed a fork from a drawer and sat down at the kitchen table.

"Thanks." I opened my container to see two enchiladas and rice waiting for me. Compared to the peaches I had earlier, this was heaven in a box.

"No problem. I figured you wouldn't have much to eat, so I thought I'd bring you something."

"I appreciate it." I waited for her to tell me why she was really here.

Three. Two. One.

"And I kind of wanted to talk to you about earlier." She said as she watched me devour my food.

Bingo. I remained silent as I shoved food into my mouth.

"I just feel bad for how we acted earlier. You're like my brother, and I'm worried about you. I don't want to lose you."

My stomach clenched as I watched her eyes fill with tears. Jade was not an emotional person, and I felt like an ass for bringing her to tears.

"Don't cry, Jade. I'm not mad at you. Honest. I promise that you aren't going to lose me."

She sniffled as she wiped away the tears that had fallen down her cheeks. "You're not my Drake anymore. I'm not sure who you are, but I know that I don't like him. I want my Drake back."

"I'm right here, Jade. Please don't cry. You're killing me."

She laughed. "You always did suck with emotions."

"You're telling me," I grumbled.

"Anyway, will you please just think about getting help? Don't do it for me or the guys or even Chloe. Do it for yourself. You're better than this."

I sighed as I put my fork down. "I know. I'm working on it, okay? I refuse to go to rehab, but I'll get my shit together for you guys. I promise."

She stood and walked around the table to stand beside me. "I hope so, Drake. If not, you're going to rip the band apart." She leaned down and kissed me on the cheek. "I'm going home, but I'll see you tomorrow. Call me if you need anything, okay?"

"Thanks, Jade. I will."

I stared at the food in front of me as she let herself out. What was I doing? How had I become this person? I hated myself for being weak. I was better than this. I shoved the food away from me. My appetite was gone. My leg started bouncing up and down as anger and disgust flooded my body. I stood up and kicked the chair away from me. It crashed to the floor, but I ignored it as I walked to the front door and threw it open. I couldn't stay here by myself tonight, or I'd go mad.

Instead of taking my car, I decided to walk to wherever my destination might be. I ended up standing in Gold's parking lot, staring at the building that I'd spent countless hours in. Maybe going back to my roots would help clear my head. My home wasn't really my home anyway. It was my uncle's house, and without Chloe there, it was nothing more than a shell of a life that I'd never have.

I shook my head to clear it and walked across the lot to the door. The usual bouncer, Jerry, was standing just inside the entrance, and he smiled when he saw me.

"Well, look who decided to grace us with his presence. Where's the rest of the band?"

"Good to see you, too, Jerry. I'm assuming they're at home, sleeping off our summer," I said as I shook his hand.

"Ah, gotcha. What brings you in here by yourself then? Where's that pretty girl of yours?"

My stomach clenched at the mention of Chloe. When I decided to come in here, it hadn't crossed my mind that the regulars wouldn't know Chloe and I weren't together anymore. That was something I didn't want to repeat over and over again.

I sighed as I ran my hand through my hair. "We're not together anymore."

Jerry's mouth dropped open. "Wait…what? Why? I figured you two would run off and get married this summer or some crazy shit like that. It seemed like you two were meant to be together."

I snorted. "Yeah, I thought so, too, until I fucked everything up."

"Dude, tell me you didn't cheat on her. If you did, I will personally kick your ass. Chloe is such a sweet girl."

"I didn't, and she is. It's complicated, and I don't want to talk about it."

He nodded. "Sorry. I didn't know. I wouldn't have brought it up if I had."

"It's fine. Listen, I'm going to grab a beer. I'll catch ya later."

"It's good to see you again. Don't be a stranger, all right?"

I nodded and turned to head to my usual table. When I found no one sitting there, I guessed it was permanently claimed by Breaking the Hunger, even after we'd been gone for months. I had barely sat down when a waitress I didn't recognize appeared beside me.

"What can I get for you?" she asked cheerfully, looking me over.

I could tell from her expression that she liked what she saw, but I wasn't interested. She was pretty, but she wasn't Chloe. I mentally smacked myself as I compared the two of them in my head. They both had platinum blonde hair and blue eyes, but that was where the similarities ended. This girl was several inches taller with an athletic build whereas Chloe was all soft edges and beautiful curves.

Who was I kidding? No one would ever compare to Chloe, physically or mentally. I'd never met someone with her spark or her love of life. Her excitement over the smallest things had always made me smile. Even now, I couldn't fight the grin turning up the corners of my lips.

The waitress apparently thought my smile was for her. Her grin widened as she leaned in closer to me. "See something you like?"

I rolled my eyes. "Yeah, I see a bar full of alcohol behind you. Bring me a beer. I don't care what kind."

She seemed a bit annoyed with me, but she kept it to herself. "Sure. Coming right up."

As she walked toward the bar, I turned my attention to the band on stage, and I immediately wished I hadn't. They sounded horrible, and that was putting it lightly. While the guy playing the guitar wasn't bad, the rest of them were. The drummer was playing faster than everyone else, and it clashed with the singer's slightly off-key singing.

I groaned as I listened to them. It was depressing to see one of our replacements. If Breaking the Hunger were playing, the bar would be packed, but tonight, there were several open tables. I wasn't being conceited, but I knew that we'd brought in a lot of business for Gold's.

A few minutes later, the waitress returned with my beer, and I sipped on it as I continued to watch the band. Someone seriously needed to remove them from the stage before people started throwing beer bottles at them. I glanced around the bar and noticed Jerry watching me with a grin on his face. I waved him over, and he laughed as he headed my way.

"They're fucking awful, aren't they?" He sat down in the chair beside me.

"Who the hell are they?" I asked.

"Some local band just starting out. I don't think any of them are older than eighteen, and they need some serious work." He paused long enough to grin at me. "Unlike you, of course. Why don't you do something acoustic when they finish up? Hopefully, this is their last song, or I'm going to stab myself in the eardrum."

I laughed at the look on his face. "I didn't bring my guitar with me."

"So? Use one of theirs. It's the least they could do after making us suffer through this."

I shrugged. "Sure. Why not?"

I needed something to help soothe my nerves, and music always served as my release when I had too much shit on my mind. Maybe it could help me now since my head was one big clusterfuck.

Sure enough, a few minutes later, the band finished their last song.

I stood and walked to the end of the stage. "Hey, do you have an acoustic guitar with you?" I asked the guitarist.

He seemed surprised, but he nodded. "Yeah, I have one out in the van."

"Do you think I could borrow it for one song?"

"Um, sure. Let me take my stuff out, and I'll bring it in for you."

I went back to my table and waited as the band packed up and carried their instruments out of the bar.

A few minutes later, the guy returned with his acoustic guitar.

"Thanks." I took the case from him and pulled out the guitar. I strummed a chord and found the instrument was horribly out of tune. I spent a couple of minutes adjusting it until I was satisfied. These guys had a lot to learn.

The bar was quiet as I left my table and went on stage. I pulled up a stool in front of the mic and sat down. "Evening, guys.

I'm sure most of you know me, but for those of you who don't, I'm Drake from Breaking the Hunger. I thought I'd play something since I'm just sitting on my ass in here."

A few people laughed, and then I started playing "Fine Again" by Seether. It seemed like the perfect song for my life right now, and I wanted to share it even if the audience wouldn't understand the meaning behind it. I let the music take over as I poured my soul into the song. This was the release I needed to deal with all the bullshit in my life. When everyone left me, music was always there to soothe me.

I finished the song and exited the stage. The room was dead silent as I handed the guitar back to its rightful owner and walked back to my table. I knew they had to be wondering what that little performance was about, and I didn't want to hang around for the questions that were sure to follow. I threw a couple of bills on the table, and without a backward glance, I left the bar to return to my own personal hell.

Chapter  3

"This is unfuckingbelievable!" Adam shouted as he boarded the label's private plane.

Jade laughed as she followed him up the steps and onto the plane. I followed behind her, and Eric entered last. We all stood in awe as we looked around the interior of the plane. The last time I had been on a plane was years ago, and it was nothing compared to this. This one was surprisingly roomy for being so small. There were five seats on each side, and in the back, two couches were situated directly in front of two flat-screen televisions mounted to the wall.

Adam ran to one of the couches and flopped down onto it. "If this is the life of a big time musician, then I never want to leave. This couch has to be worth more than my car!"

I couldn't help but grin as I slid down into one of the seats. I could always count on Adam to cheer me up when I was having a shitty day. Jade sat down in the aisle across from me, and Eric took the seat in front of me.

"I have to admit that this is pretty cool," Eric said as he looked at me.

"Yeah, it is. I could get used to this," Jade said.

After spending over an hour and a half in Eric's cramped car on the drive to the Pittsburgh International Airport, these seats felt like heaven on earth. I stretched my legs out in front of me and reclined the seat.

"It is a pretty nice setup," I said before yawning.

I'd tossed and turned most of the night before as Chloe had constantly filled my mind. I'd wondered how close was she to me? What would she do if I called her and asked to come over? Would she hang up on me? Would she let me spend the night with her? Of course she wouldn't. That was a stupid question. She'd made her decision very clear. As long as I was using, she didn't want anything to do with me. I wasn't sure if she would even talk to me once I was clean.

When she wasn't consuming my thoughts, I was thinking about how many hours had passed since I used last. This was the longest I'd gone without coke for a while, and I felt like I was going crazy. I was determined to stop using though. I was tired of hurting everyone around me, but I wasn't sure how long I could handle it.

I didn't want the band to know that I was trying to stop on my own. They would only worry about me and watch me constantly. I didn't need three babysitters. I could do this on my own.

And if you fail, they'll never even know you tried, a little voice in my head said.

I had to agree with it. If I couldn't quit on my own, I didn't want to see the disappointment written all over their faces.

"Attention, passengers. We are preparing for takeoff. Please make sure your seat belts are fastened," a male voice said over the intercom.

I fastened my seat belt as Adam stood from the couch and walked to the nearest seat.

I had to admit that I was excited about this whole thing. If the label liked us, it would change our entire lives. We could get a deal, record an album, and tour the country. There would be no more gigs in small-town bars for us. I smiled as I pictured myself in front of thousands of fans with Chloe standing just offstage, watching me proudly with a huge grin on her face.

And there she was again. She obviously didn't miss me, so why couldn't I get her out of my head? Thoughts of her consumed me. She was an addiction, just like the cocaine, and I couldn't let either one of them go.

A young woman stepped out of the cockpit and started walking toward us. She checked to make sure each of our seat belts were secured before walking back into the cabin. I closed my eyes and listened to Adam and Jade bicker as we waited for the plane to take off.

A few minutes later, I opened my eyes to see the same woman from earlier walking back into our cabin. She took a seat in the front. "We will be taking off momentarily."

Sure enough, less than a minute later, I felt the plane start to move. I grabbed both armrests, preparing myself for when we lifted off the runway. Flying didn't scare me, but I wasn't too keen on the actual takeoff part. When I felt the plane leaving the ground, the muscles in my arms tightened as I clung to the armrests. I closed my eyes and waited for the okay to unfasten my seat belt.

When the pilot announced that we could move around the cabin, I threw off my seat belt and stood. Between craving my fix and the takeoff, I was feeling antsy to say the least. I walked to the couches and dropped myself down on one of them. Maybe I could nap for a little bit if I closed my eyes and blocked out the voices in the cabin.

I opened my eyes and looked around. I noticed Eric studying me closely. Lately, it seemed like he was always watching me, and it made me nervous. Eric was one of the most perceptive people I had ever known, and his constant scrutiny made me feel like he could see right into me.

He stood and headed toward me. He sat down beside me and stared at the blank television screen. He obviously wanted to talk, but I wasn't sure if he was waiting for me to say something or if he was thinking things over before he spoke.

"You okay?" Eric finally asked.

"Yeah, I'm fine. Why?"

"You're fidgety today, more than normal." He looked away from the television and directed his gaze at me.

"Flying makes me nervous," I lied.

"It's more than that. Did you see Chloe last night or something?" he asked.

That wasn't what I had expected at all. He never mentioned Chloe. "No, I didn't. I know when I'm not wanted, and I'm not about to go chase after her like a lovesick idiot."

"You still love her."

It wasn't a question. He was simply stating the obvious, but for some reason, it bothered me.

"Does it matter?" I asked.

"It does."

"It doesn't. Even if I do still love her, she's made it clear that she wants nothing to do with me."

"She left because she loves you, Drake. She couldn't stand to watch you destroy yourself. You have to know that."

I shrugged, hoping that he would drop the conversation. Of course, I knew he wouldn't though. Eric rarely spoke about private matters, so when he did, he made sure to say everything he needed to.

"If this label signs us, things are going to change. If you think the women are bad now, just wait. You will have hundreds of women throwing themselves at you constantly."

"So? What are you trying to get at?"

"I honestly think Chloe would take you back in a heartbeat if you got your life together. I just don't want you to do anything that you might regret later."

"Like sleep with one of the groupies?" I asked, finally understanding what he was getting at.

"Exactly. You're a good guy, Drake, and I hate seeing you like this. I don't want you to destroy what you had with Chloe any more than you already have. Just think things through before you act."

I nodded. "I will."

He smacked me on the back as he stood from the couch. "Good to hear."

I relaxed as I watched him walk back up to the front toward Jade and Adam. His words echoed through my mind. Even though I realized that Chloe wasn't coming back, I hadn't accepted any invitations from the women who threw themselves at me while I had been out at the bars. It had just felt wrong to me, like I would be cheating. Besides, no woman could ever come close to Chloe. She was one in a billion.

The rest of the flight was uneventful. I felt like I hadn't slept in weeks, but no matter how hard I tried, sleep wouldn't come. All I wanted was a line of coke and to get off this damn plane. That wasn't too much to ask, was it? By the time we landed in L.A., I was cranky and ready to put my fist through a wall.

I followed the rest of the band off the plane and into the airport. We collected our bags and walked toward the exit. Near the door, we noticed a huge guy holding a sign with our names on it. Eric approached him first, and we all followed. After the guy verified who we were, he led us outside to a limo idling by the curb.

I whistled as I slid into the seat next to Jade. Eric and Adam slid in across from us. This label was the real deal. First, they had flown us over in a private plane, and now, we were in their limo. We rode in silence. All of us seemed too nervous to say anything. When the limo stopped, I glanced out the window to see a huge building with the record label's name displayed across the entrance.

The driver opened the door and waited as we all exited the car. Then, he led us up the steps and into the lobby. From the pristine marble floors to the glass reception desk, the place screamed money. We walked down a short hallway to a row of elevators. As soon as the doors opened, the driver ushered us in before he stepped inside. The doors closed, and he pressed the button for the eighteenth floor. I stared at my reflection in the door as we were lifted up.

My hands were sweating from nerves, and I wiped them repeatedly on my jeans. I wasn't one to get nervous, but my future depended on the decisions of the people working in this building. We would either be set for life or thrown out like trash.

The elevator dinged, and the doors slid open to reveal a brightly lit hallway. The driver, who had yet to speak to any of us except for Eric at the airport, led us down the hallway to a door at the very end. After knocking loudly, he swung the door open and walked in with us following right behind him.

"Mr. Sanders, I have the band you requested," he said in a deep voice that matched his scary-as-fuck appearance.

I took a closer look at him and frowned. If I saw this guy on the street, I would have gone out of my way to avoid him. Even though he was dressed in a suit, I could see tattoos peeking out of the collar and sleeves of his shirt. His head was shaved, and with the added benefit of him being well over six feet tall, he was one scary bastard.

"Excellent! Thank you for your assistance, Alex. I'll take it from here," a voice said from across the room.

I looked up to see a middle-aged man sitting at a desk. He was the exact opposite of Alex. He was also dressed in a suit, but that was the only similarity between the two men. Desk guy had a small build with thinning hair and wrinkles around his eyes and across his forehead.

"It's a pleasure to meet all of you. We loved the demo tape you sent, and I personally can't wait to hear what you can do in our studio."

"Uh, thank you, Mr.—" Eric started.

"Oh, of course. How silly of me. I'm Brad Sanders. I spoke with you on the phone the other day."

"Right, well, it's nice to officially meet you, Mr. Sanders," Eric said.

"The pleasure is all mine. Please call me Brad. We will be spending a good bit of time with each other, so there's no need for formalities." He smiled at us.

"All right then. I'm Eric. This is Adam, Jade, and Drake."

Brad stood, walked over to us, and shook each of our hands. He seemed like a nice guy, but I wasn't one to trust others, and I refused to fall for the nice-guy act. Guys like him used bands all the time. Until he could prove to me that he wasn't a dick, I wasn't ready to like him. Sure, I had to be polite, but that didn't mean I had to like it.

"Why don't all of you take a seat? Then, I'll go over some things with you. I'm sure Eric filled you in on the phone conversation we had a couple of days ago."

We all nodded as we took the seats surrounding the desk.

"Good. All right, let's get down to business. As I said before, we absolutely loved your demo. You all have amazing potential, and with our help, I think your band could be the next big thing in the rock world. We want you to record a few of your current songs in our studio, and we'll see how things go. If you're as good as you sounded on the CD you sent in, we'll want to sign you."

"And if you don't?" I asked, wanting to make him squirm.

He gave me a false cheery smile. "Don't think we are just going to abandon you. I have no doubt that you have raw potential. In the end, if we can't come to an agreement, I will personally pay for your trip home."

I nodded, satisfied with his answer.

"While you are here, we have booked rooms for each of you in a hotel not far from here, so you are easily accessible to us. By now, I'm sure you know that recording music is not easy, even recording on your own. You will spend several hours a day in our studio, working with the best team money can buy."

"And you guys are paying for our rooms and making sure we have everything we need?" Adam asked.

"Of course! We asked you to come here. You won't need to spend a dime while you're here."

"Fucking sweet!" Adam said.

Brad laughed as Jade rolled her eyes.

"Yes, it is a very sweet deal. I'm sure you're all tired, so I don't expect you to jump right into the studio today. Alex will take you to the hotel, and he will pick you up at eight o'clock sharp tomorrow morning. Get a good night's rest. Tomorrow we get to work."

We all stood, thanked him, and walked to the door. Alex was standing just down the hallway, waiting for us. We followed him back to the elevators, and once we were back on the first floor, we headed outside and got back into the limo. The ride to the hotel was short since it was only a few blocks away from the label. It seemed they really did want to keep us close.

Alex parked the limo, and almost instantly, he opened the door for us to exit. He helped the hotel staff unload our bags from the back of the car. Afterward, he turned to us. "Your rooms are listed under your names." He handed Eric a piece of paper. "If you need anything, this is my number. I will see you all in the morning." With that, he stepped away from us and got back into the limo.

That guy had the personality of a gnat. I wasn't sure if he was an arrogant ass by nature or if he just didn't like us. Either way, I didn't like him.

We walked inside, and I instantly felt uncomfortable. The hotel was as fancy as the building we had just left. I wasn't used to high-class places, and this place was as high-class as they came. At the reception desk, we checked in and got directions to our rooms. We rode the elevator up with a hotel employee and helped him unload our bags outside each of our rooms. I tipped him twenty dollars, and he looked at me like I was nuts. I shrugged as I glanced at Adam as the employee walked down the hallway. I'd seriously overpaid or underpaid the guy. Oh well, I didn't give a shit either way.

We agreed to meet later in Eric's room after we each went to our own rooms to unpack. I slid my key card into the lock and swung the door open to reveal a massive room. While I knew it couldn't be the nicest room in this hotel, it was insane to me. Any hotel I'd slept in before came with a bed and a bathroom only, but this place had it all—a bed, bathroom, couch, desk, and even a small kitchen. The label had obviously planned to keep us here for a while. Too bad I couldn't cook to save my life. If Chloe were here, she'd be jumping up and down in excitement.

I squeezed my eyes shut, trying to block thoughts of her from my mind. It wasn't fair. No matter where I was or what I was doing, she was always there. Every single thing I saw reminded me of her.

I threw my bag on the bed and unzipped it to start putting things away in the dresser across from the bed. I honestly hadn't expected to be here for long, so I'd only brought enough clothes for a week. I hoped a Laundromat was close by or maybe the hotel had some service to wash my clothes. After I put all my clothes away, I took my toiletries to the bathroom and tossed my empty bag against the far wall.

Well, it wasn't completely empty. There was one small compartment that I hadn't yet opened. Just in case, I'd stashed a bag of coke in there. I'd taken a chance with airport security when we were still in Pittsburgh, and lucky for me, we had skipped through security since we were on a private plane. Now, I wished that I hadn't brought it with me. I sat down on the bed and stared at my bag. It seemed like the coke was calling out to me, begging me to get my fix.

I fell back onto the bed and stared at the ceiling. I wished that Chloe were here with me.

With her, maybe it would be easier to ignore the screaming voice in my head. *To hell with the rest of the world. Do what you want.*

Maybe if she'd stuck by me, I'd be clean by now. Yeah, I knew I would be. It was all her fault that I was still trapped in this hell. If she'd really cared, she would have stayed to make sure I was okay. Instead, she'd left me behind without a second thought. She didn't care about me. The only person she cared about was herself. Needing to hit something, I slammed my fists on the bed.

It did little to soothe my temper. Instead, I felt angrier. How could she do that to me? She had left me, just left me. I fucking hated her, and I hated the fact that I still loved her. Damn her! Damn it all!

I stood up and stomped across the room to my bag. I sat it on the desk and unzipped the compartment that had all the answers. I was so sick of dealing with my fucked up emotions all the time. I just wanted that release, that world of pleasure where nothing mattered. There was no label, there was no Chloe, there were no dead parents, and most importantly, there was no pain. Fuck it all. No, fuck *them* all.

I pulled the bag and my trusty mirror out and walked to the couch to sit down. I'd stocked up only a few days ago, and I knew I had enough to last me a week or two. I set the mirror on the table and dumped some of the powder onto it. After pulling my credit card and a bill out of my wallet, I crushed up the coke and separated it into two lines. I rolled the bill and leaned down, but then I stopped at the last second. Was I really giving up this soon? Hadn't I just decided last night that I was done with this? I was destroying everything for myself and everyone around me.

I stared down at the powder and willed myself to take it to the bathroom and flush it down the toilet. But I couldn't do it. I needed it too much. I couldn't deal with life without some kind of release, and this was the best thing that I had right now. I lowered my head once again and snorted both of the lines, one right after the other. I threw the bill down on the table as I leaned back

41

against the couch. I felt half-disgusted with myself and half-happy now that I knew my release was so close.

I closed my eyes and waited for the effects to take over. A few minutes later, I started to feel them, and I breathed a sigh of relief. Yes, this was what I wanted, what I needed. I could handle this. I wouldn't let it control me. The guys and Jade were worried over nothing. How could something that felt this good ever be bad? It helped me focus, which is what I needed. When I didn't have it, I always felt rage bubbling to the surface, and I lost control. That would be when everyone needed to worry, not when I felt like this.

I smiled to myself as I stood and grabbed my key card off the table. It was time to meet up with everyone in Eric's room. I closed the door behind me and walked down the hall to his room. I knocked, and a few seconds later, Eric opened the door to let me in.

He took one look at me and shook his head. "Really?" he asked.

"What?"

"You're high, Drake. I thought you were trying to work on it."

"I am," I said defensively. "This is the first time today. That's almost twenty-four hours. I don't know what you're so worried about anyway. You hate when I get all pissed off, don't you? I never feel that way after I've snorted a line."

"No, but you're a raging dick when it starts to wear off," Adam said from the couch.

I flipped him off as I sat down next to him. "Fuck you. I'm fine, and I'm not using as much as I was. At least I'm trying, so back off."

"Whatever," Adam growled. "I wish Chloe were here. She'd rip off your dick for this shit."

For the first time ever, I snapped while I was high. I grabbed the neck of his shirt and drew my arm back to punch him in the face.

Eric grabbed my arm and pulled me away from Adam. "That's it!" he shouted.

I froze. Eric never shouted.

"You need to get your shit together, or you're going to be on your own. I can't watch you destroy yourself and attack us every chance you get," Eric said.

Adam adjusted his shirt and stood. "If it wasn't for this label wanting us, I'd vote to kick your ass out right now. I'm so sick of it."

"Don't you ever fucking bring up Chloe like that again! She left me, just like you guys want to. If she were still here, I wouldn't be in this mess!"

"So, you admit that you're in over your head?" Eric asked.

"What? No! I just meant—"

"We know what you meant. Deny it all you want, but you need help," Adam said as he walked to the door. He glanced back at Eric. "I'm out of here before I beat his head in."

He slammed the door, leaving me alone with Eric. I ran my hands through my hair. I was at a loss for words. I had this under control, regardless of what they thought.

"You've lost control, Drake. I wish you could see that. You're like a brother to me. As far as I'm concerned, you *are* my brother and it's killing me to watch you go through this alone. I wish you would let us help you," Eric said.

"I don't need your help or anyone else's. I've taken care of myself my entire life, and that isn't going to change."

"But you're not alone, and I wish you could see that. Jade, Adam, and I all love you. Chloe does, too, even if she isn't here to tell you."

"You guys are my family, and I know you care, but you're worrying over nothing. I wish you'd just leave me alone."

"We aren't going to leave you alone until you get help. You've got Jade scared to death. She's afraid to even leave you on your own. A little bit ago, she came over here, and she was freaking out and worried about what you would do since you have a room to yourself." He gave me a pointed look. "Obviously, she was right."

"I'm not dealing with this right now. I'm going back to my room." I stood and walked to the door. I was so sick of this shit. I wanted my friends back, not these crazy people who wouldn't leave me alone.

I spent the rest of the night locked up in my room. Someone came to my door and knocked a few times. After hearing

44

obscenities being shouted at me from the other side, I knew it was Jade, but I ignored her. She tried calling me a few times, but I ignored those as well. I just wanted to be alone.

It was well after midnight when I picked up my phone and started flipping through some of my pictures. I started with the first picture I had ever taken of Chloe and continued to go through them until I reached the last one. It had been taken only days before she'd left me. She had fallen asleep while we were on the bus, and I'd snapped picture after picture of her as she slept peacefully in my bunk. I'd thought that we'd be together forever, but as usual, things never worked out the way I'd planned. If I had known that she would be gone so soon after that, I would have crawled into that small bunk and held her tight.

I just hoped that she hadn't run back to Jordan or Logan. I wasn't sure how I would handle it if I ever saw her with either of them. She was mine even if she didn't think so anymore, and I didn't want Jordan or Logan touching her, kissing her, or holding her at night. As I imagined either of them in bed with her, I felt like I'd been punched in the stomach. Her body and soul were supposed to be mine and mine alone.

I plugged my phone in to charge it, and I threw the covers back on my bed. I had a huge day tomorrow, and I needed to get some sleep. I tossed and turned, unable to put my mind to rest. Now that the thought had popped into my head, all I could see was Chloe in bed with someone else. The picture Kadi had shown me of Chloe and Jordan in bed together was what had started all of this, and here I was again, going through the same hell as before.

Chapter 4

I had finally managed to fall asleep around three in the morning, and when the alarm went off at six, I wanted to shoot myself. I barely managed to crawl out of bed and make it to the bathroom to turn on the shower. I wasn't a morning person, and the time difference was really screwing with me. I stripped out of my boxers and stepped into the hot water. I just stood there as I let it fall around me. The heat and the water beating against my skin slowly started to wake me up. I stayed in there for far longer than necessary before stepping out and toweling off.

After getting dressed and ordering room service for breakfast, I walked to Eric's room and knocked on the door. He opened it, looking tired.

"Rough night?" I asked as I walked into his room.

"Well, with Jade being here until well after midnight, it was kind of hard to sleep," he grumbled.

"Oh," I said, unsure of how to respond to that.

"Yeah, oh. She was worried sick about you when she found out what happened. She wanted to call the main desk and have them check on you, but I wouldn't let her. That's just what we need—the hotel informing Brad that we have a drug addict as the front man, and we were afraid he overdosed."

"I wouldn't overdose, dumbass."

"You wouldn't do it on purpose, but if you were pissed and decided to take more…well, you don't know what could happen."

I counted to ten in my head to keep my cool. "Let's not start the day off by talking about this, okay? We have too much shit to get done."

"You're right, but I'm still pissed at you."

"When aren't you lately?" I grinned at him.

He shot me a dirty look. "I'm always pissed at you, and you can blame yourself for that."

Someone knocked on the door, and he went to answer it. Jade and Adam were both standing on the other side. When Jade saw me, she pushed past Eric and ran toward me.

"Thank God! Why didn't you answer your phone?" she asked, hugging me.

I shrugged as she released me from her death grip. "I just wanted to be alone for a while."

"I was worried sick about you, Drake. Please don't do that to me again."

"I won't. I promise." I smiled at her.

"I'm holding you to that." She frowned.

"I promised, didn't I? Now, let's get going. I'm sure Adam is waiting on us by now."

"Let's go." Taking my hand, Jade led me out of the room and to the elevators. She didn't let go until we were sitting in the back of the limo on our way to the studio.

Brad had told Eric that we wouldn't need our instruments for the recording sessions because the studio had several to pick from. While I knew they would have the best of the best, it still made me uneasy to think I'd be playing a guitar that I wasn't used to.

This morning, I'd decided to leave my stash in my room. I was sure that I'd be fine without it for a few hours, and I wanted to make sure that I gave the band everything I had. They deserved nothing less. I tried to pay attention to whatever Jade was saying, but I was failing miserably. My mind was on overload from the stress of the entire situation.

I glanced over at Adam, who had been suspiciously quiet since I saw him in Eric's room. He was staring out the window, ignoring all of us. I wasn't sure if he was nervous or if he was still mad at me over last night. Either way, his silence bothered me.

I waited until we were out of the limo and walking into the building before I approached him.

"Everything okay with you? I don't think you've ever been this quiet."

"Just peachy," Adam said as he shoved past me.

Well, all right then. He was obviously still mad at me. I rolled my eyes as I followed the rest of the group into the elevator. He'd get over it soon enough. Now was not the time to be fighting among ourselves. We had a job to do, and we needed to do it well.

When we reached Brad's office, Alex knocked on the door.

Brad opened it instantly, smiling at all of us. "You're right on time. Follow me, and I'll take you down to the studio."

I raised an eyebrow. Wouldn't it have been simpler for Alex to take us to the studio? Oh well, Brad was the boss, and if he wanted to play musical elevators, then I would do it.

After yet another elevator ride that took us to the basement level of the building, we stepped out to see a massive recording studio. My mouth dropped open as I looked around. After recording most of our stuff in Eric's garage, this setup was out of this world.

There were a few people sitting around a control panel just outside of the recording studio. They all looked up as Brad led us over to them.

He stopped in front of them. "Good morning, gentlemen. I'd like to introduce you to the band you will be working with today. This is Eric, Adam, Jade, and Drake."

I was surprised when he named each of us off. I figured guys like him forgot names as soon as the faces were out of sight.

"I'm Frank, and this is Tony and Eddy. It's nice to meet you guys," the oldest of the group said as he shook each of our hands.

"You guys can go on in, and then we can get started. For today, we're going to focus on a few of the songs you sent to us. Basically, we want to see what you can do right out of the gates. If that goes well and Brad gives us the go-ahead, we will start cutting tracks for the first album," Tony said.

"Sounds good to me," I said.

I walked into the studio, and the rest of the band followed me. They each took their respective places. The guys in the control room gave us a few minutes, so we could make sure our instruments were tuned. I gave them the okay when we were ready to go.

Frank's voice came over the speakers in the room. "There are a few songs we want to hear today. The first one is 'Whirlwind.' Let's do that one now."

My heart dropped to my stomach. "Whirlwind" was a song I'd written about Chloe when she was still with Logan. Of course that would be the first song they wanted to record. Even here, thousands of miles away from her, people continued to taunt me with her presence—or rather, her lack of presence.

"Everything okay?" Frank asked.

"Uh, yeah. We're ready when you are," I said, trying to think of anything else besides *her*.

The red light in front of me came on, and I waited as Jade started the song with a slow beat. Adam and Eric waited until it was their time, and then they began to play. I closed my eyes as I started belting out the lyrics to the song that brought me so much pain.

I wasn't sure what it was,
What you did to me.
I felt myself change.

Something shifted when I looked into your eyes,
Engulfing me in flames,
Burning me to the core.

But it wasn't meant to be.
You see, you and I,
We're a whirlwind,
Destroying everything in our path.

But isn't that what love does?
It makes us weak, far from free.
I gave you everything, and you turned it back on me.
You turned it back on me.

We finished the song, and I opened my eyes to see the guys, including Brad, in the other room, watching us with their mouths hanging open. At least someone liked me today.

The red light turned off, and Brad's voice came over the speakers. "That was incredible! It's been a long time since anyone has shocked me, but you guys have managed to do it. Why don't you do 'Fire' next?"

I nodded, and the red light came on again.

We spent the rest of the day singing song after song, only breaking once or twice for lunch and smoke breaks. By the time evening rolled around, I was on edge and snapping at everyone, including Brad. All I wanted to do was go back to my hotel room and snort a line or two.

When Brad announced that we were done for the day, I almost started fist-pumping. As soon as we were out of the studio and in the control room though, he stopped us. I debated on how bad it would look if I shoved him out of the way, but then I decided I could hold out for a few minutes before I did anything drastic.

"You guys were incredible. I have a meeting in the morning, so catch a few extra hours of sleep tonight. Alex will pick you up around ten tomorrow morning. I have a few things I want to discuss with you, so just come up to my office when you get here."

"Sure thing," Jade said.

Brad stepped aside to let us go, and Alex appeared to guide us out of the building and drive us back to the hotel.

I nearly ran to my room when Alex dropped us off. Jade stopped me to ask if I wanted to go out for dinner, but I lied and told her I was too tired and that I'd just have something sent to my room. I just wanted to escape her. She seemed disappointed, but she didn't question me. I told them all good night and hurried to my room.

After I locked the dead bolt on the door, I walked to my bag and pulled out my stash. I sat down on the couch, and then I dumped some of the powder onto my mirror and proceeded with my usual routine. Without a second thought, I snorted the lines I'd made. Even though today had been amazing, I was stressed and needed to relax more than anything. From now on, I'd keep something with me just in case.

As I started feeling the effects from using cocaine, I walked to my bed and fell onto it. I just lay there as the tension left my body.

I must have passed out because I awoke later to the sound of someone beating the shit out of my door. I groaned as I stood and walked to the door. I threw it open to see Adam, Eric, and Jade all standing there, looking grumpy.

"What's up?" I asked before yawning.

"We've been calling you and beating on this damn door for half an hour. We're supposed to be downstairs in ten minutes! Go shower and get dressed," Adam growled.

I glanced at the clock on the wall, and my eyes widened. "Shit!"

"Yeah, shit. We'll be waiting downstairs. Don't fuck around," Jade said.

As they turned away, I shut the door. I ran to the bathroom and jumped into the shower. After taking the fastest shower on record, I ran to the dresser and threw on clean clothes. I grabbed my stuff and ran for the door, hoping that the others hadn't left without me. Normally, it wouldn't be a concern, but they had been so pissed at me lately, so I wasn't sure if they'd wait or not. If they had left, I could at least walk to the studio since it wasn't that far.

When the elevator opened on the ground floor, I took off running across the lobby. Several people threw dirty looks my way, but I ignored them. I made it outside just as the limo was pulling up to the curb. The rest of the band looked relieved as we all got into it.

"I was starting to wonder if you'd make it," Eric said as we pulled away from the hotel.

"I did but just barely. I knew you'd leave me, so I hurried."

"We wouldn't have left you, you idiot. It would be kind of hard to record anything if our vocalist was missing." Jade said as she rolled her eyes.

I hadn't thought of that. I was the most important part of the band. Without me, half of our fans wouldn't even know who we were. I was the face of Breaking the Hunger, and everyone in this limo knew it. They could threaten to kick me out, but in the end, I knew they wouldn't do it. They'd tank if I left.

When I chuckled to myself, Jade looked at me like I'd lost my mind.

"What are you laughing at?" she asked.

"Oh, nothing. Just thinking about a funny joke," I lied.

"Okay then," she said. I ignored the strange look she gave me.

After the limo pulled up to the building, we got out and headed inside. Alex didn't accompany us up to Brad's office this time. He must have figured we wouldn't get lost at this point. When Eric knocked on the door, Brad opened it almost immediately and stepped back to let us in. I took a seat in the same chair where I had sat last time.

Brad walked around his desk and sat down. "Right on time. I just finished up my meeting a few minutes ago." He smiled at us.

This guy sure seemed to smile a lot.

"Actually, the meeting was about the four of you."

I raised a brow but said nothing, and the rest of the band remained silent as well.

"Don't look so worried. The meeting went well. I played the main guys upstairs some of what we recorded yesterday, and every single person there loved it. I know this seems kind of fast, but we want to sign you."

I sat straight up in my seat. "Wait, wait, wait. You're telling me that after only one day of listening to us play, you want to sign us?"

"That's what I just said. All of you have amazing talent, but especially you, Drake. There's just something about your voice that draws others in. I haven't heard anything like it in a long time."

"What happens now?" Jade asked.

"If you accept our offer, we'll give you the contracts to look over. After you sign, we'll figure out which of your current songs to put on your first album, and then we'll start working on a song to release to the radio stations. Soon after that, I'd also like to do a music video for your first single. We need to get your faces out to the public. You're all attractive, and that will get you a fan base just as fast as your music."

"What kind of time frame are we looking at—from when we sign the contract until the album is released?" Eric asked.

"It will take a few months to get everything ready. Considering it's late September now, I'd like to have the first single out right after Christmas. Sales are usually down in January since everyone is broke from Christmas, but if we release it on the radio and online, we can at least start a fan base. Once we have that, we'll plan for the album to be ready by late spring or early summer. That way, we can promote you guys for a while. The fact that you already have enough songs for two albums will help speed up the process."

I just sat there and stared at him. This was it. Our big break was finally here. After years of playing together, we'd finally done it. My lips turned up as I let that sink in.

Brad continued to talk, going through all the details of our contract. Brad mentioned the amount of our advance when Adam was taking a drink from his bottle of water. He started choking, and Eric had to beat him on the back.

"Holy shit!" Adam shouted when he could finally speak.

Brad laughed at Adam. "Yes, we have been very generous with your advance, but we feel that you will be worth it."

"Can we have a few minutes alone to talk this over?" Eric asked.

"Certainly. I need to run upstairs for a minute. Talk among yourselves while I'm gone."

After Brad left his office, Eric turned to us. "What do you guys think?"

Jade grinned. "I say yes! How could we say no to that?"

"I'm in, too," Adam said.

All eyes turned to me. "I'm in, too. Jade's right. There's no way we can turn down that kind of offer."

"All right then. I just wanted to make sure we all agreed." Eric smiled. "This is it, guys!"

"It is!" Jade shouted as she did a little dance in her chair.

There was a knock on the door, and a few seconds later, Brad stepped back into the room. "Did I give you enough time?"

"Yes, we're ready to sign," Eric said.

"Excellent! I have the contracts on my desk." Brad walked around us and picked up a folder from the top of his desk. "Here we are. Feel free to read everything over before you sign, but I've given you most of the details."

He handed each of us a set of papers, and I started reading through mine. I sucked with legal wording, but as far as I could tell, everything was exactly as he'd said. I grabbed a pen from his desk and signed my name on the line at the bottom of the last page.

There—it was done. Adrenaline shot through me as I handed the document back to Brad. With that contract, our fates were sealed. I wanted to jump out of my chair and start running around the room. My leg started bouncing, and I had to force myself to sit still. I had so much adrenaline running through my body, and I couldn't take it anymore. I had to move.

"Do you mind if I use the restroom?" I asked, finding an excuse to leave.

"Not at all. It's right down the hall on the left," Brad said.

I ignored the look Adam gave me before I slipped out of the office. I started walking down the hallway, and then I saw the restroom only a few doors away from Brad's office, just like he'd said.

I pushed open the door and walked inside to see the restroom was even fancy. These people were really over the top. The sinks and floor were both made out of a beautiful black marble. A black leather couch was in the far corner, and the urinals were on the opposite wall. There were three black stalls next to them. I walked into one, almost expecting the toilets to be made out of gold.

I was relieved when I saw that they had at least left the toilets alone. I closed the lid and sat down. I pulled my bag and mirror from my pocket and started pouring the powder onto it. I made my lines and snorted them quickly. I wasn't sure why I was snorting right now. I wasn't upset or anything, but I just wanted to.

Call it my private celebration—sitting on a toilet in a restroom stall. Yeah, apparently, I'd sunk that low.

Someone walked into the bathroom, and I quickly threw everything back into my pocket. I flushed the toilet and stepped out of the stall to see some guy in a suit at one of the urinals. I ignored him as I left the restroom and walked back down the hall to Brad's office. When I walked in, Brad and the others were holding up glasses.

"Just in time, Drake! We're celebrating our partnership!" Brad handed me a glass.

I clinked my glass against theirs and took a sip of whatever was inside. I almost gagged as the taste of champagne hit my tongue. I never understood how people could stand to drink this crap. I looked around to see Jade wincing as she sipped, but Eric and Adam didn't seem to be bothered by the taste. They could have at it. That stuff was nasty.

I set my mostly full glass on Brad's desk. He didn't seem to notice it when he set his empty glass next to it.

"All right, let's go down to the studio and get some work done," Brad said.

We all followed him out of his office and to the elevators. As soon as we hit the basement floor, he instructed us to go into the studio and get ready. My head was spinning a little, and I tripped over a cable as I was walking toward the door.

"You okay there, buddy?" Tony asked, looking at me with concern.

60

"Yeah, I'm fine." I shook my head to clear it.

I still felt a little weird, but I ignored it as I took my place and picked up the guitar sitting next to the mic stand. It seemed to be tuned good enough, so I waited as Jade, Eric, and Adam adjusted their instruments.

When they gave the okay, Brad's voice came over the speakers. "Let's do 'Whirlwind' again. I'm going to have you play it a few times, and then we'll work through whatever needs changed."

I groaned to myself. Of course that was the song they wanted to start with again. The red light came on a few seconds later, and I waited as first Jade and then Eric and Adam entered the song. When it was my turn, I started singing. I still felt a little dizzy, but I tried to ignore it.

I made it halfway through the song before I had to stop. The room was spinning around me, and as I tried to put the mic in its stand, I lost my balance. In what seemed like slow motion, I fell to the floor, and I heard Jade shouting my name.

The next thing I knew, Adam was shaking me. I groaned as I tried to sit up. My head felt like it was splitting open.

"Stay down for a minute. You hit your head when you fell," Jade said, leaning over me.

"It fucking hurts." I lifted a hand to touch the back of my head. Luckily, there was no blood when I pulled it away.

"Your head is too hard to be hurt," Adam grumbled as he helped me stand.

Jade glared at him as she wrapped her arm around me to help support my weight. The room was still spinning, and I stumbled. Adam caught me as I started to fall again, and Jade grunted as my weight nearly caused her to fall.

Out of nowhere, Brad appeared in front of me. "You all right there, Drake?"

"I'm fine. I'm just dizzy."

"Why don't you sit down for a while? It might help," Jade said.

She and Adam helped me out of the studio and into the control room. They sat me down in a chair next to the soundboard.

When I closed my eyes, the spinning got even worse. "This fucking sucks," I groaned.

"Has he eaten today?" Tony asked with concern.

"I don't think so. We were running late this morning," Jade said, patting my knee.

Tony picked up the phone and ordered someone to bring me a can of soda and whatever food they could find. "There. They will have it down here in a few minutes," he said as he hung up.

"Thanks," I mumbled.

I was still dizzy when my food arrived. I choked down whatever it was and chugged my soda.

Jade hovered around me with a concerned look on her face. "Are you still dizzy?"

"I am, but I'll be fine. Quit acting like a mother hen." I leaned down and rested my head in my hands.

"Maybe we should call it a day. Let's get Drake back to the hotel, so he can rest," Brad said. He pulled out his phone and called Alex to come and pick us up.

My bed sounded heavenly right about now. Between the headache and the dizziness, I wasn't sure I could stand, let alone sing. Eric and Adam helped me up and led me to the elevators. Jade promised Brad she'd call later to let him know how I was doing, and then we rode up to the first floor.

Once we made it back to the hotel, the guys helped me out of the limo and up to my room. They all but tossed me onto the bed as all three of them circled around me.

"Thanks for helping me, guys. I'm going to try to get some sleep. Maybe that will help," I said, looking up at them.

"Do you want something for your head? Is it safe for you to even take anything with cocaine in your system?" Jade asked angrily.

I was not in the mood for this right now. "I'm fine. I just need to sleep."

"No, you need to stop using. This is getting out of hand!" Jade shouted.

"No, it's already been out of hand for a while," Eric said, staring down at me.

"Just leave me the fuck alone right now, okay? I'm not in the mood to fight with you guys!" I yelled.

"Whatever. I'm so sick of this shit," Adam growled.

"We all are. Drake, please get help before you kill yourself," Jade pleaded.

"Get. Out," I said in a deadly quiet voice that I'd never used with Jade.

"Talking to you is like talking to a brick wall!" She stomped her foot.

If I wasn't so pissed, I would have laughed at her.

"What would Chloe say if she saw you like this? Maybe I should text her and tell her exactly what is going on instead of sugarcoating everything for her."

I sat straight up in the bed. "You've been talking to Chloe?"

Her eyes widened as she realized what she'd said. "I…uh—"

"You have! What did she say? How is she?" I asked. I had to know how she was. If Jade had mentioned that she was still talking to Chloe before this, I would have been bugging her daily for updates. Instead, I'd spent the last two-and-a-half months going mad, wondering what she was up to.

"She's okay. She checks in every once in a while to see how you are. She knows that you're still using, but she doesn't know how bad it is. She's worried to death about you."

She was worried about me. That brought me more happiness than I wanted to admit. I was afraid that she'd already moved on and forgotten about me.

"Amber has forced her to go on a few dates, but she's not over you yet."

And there went my happiness. Chloe was dating again. It didn't matter that Jade had said Chloe wasn't over me. She was trying to move on with someone else.

"With who? Logan? Jordan?" I asked.

"I have no idea who it is, but I don't think it's either of them. From what she's told me, I think they're guys Amber knows from around campus."

I wanted to kill Amber for pushing Chloe to move on. I knew Amber was just being a good friend, but I didn't want Chloe to give up on me. If she kept dating, she would eventually find some asshole who actually deserved her, and any hope that I had of winning her back would be gone.

"Can you guys please leave me alone?" I asked.

"I didn't mean to upset you. It just slipped out," Jade said.

"I'm not upset. I just want to sleep right now," I lied.

"If you're sure—" she said.

"I am."

Adam and Jade left the room, but Eric stayed behind. I groaned as I rolled over until my back was facing him. Maybe he would take the hint and leave.

"Why don't you focus on what Jade just told you? Maybe that will help you deal with this."

"What? The fact that Chloe is dating other guys? Yeah, that'll perk my mood right up," I said sarcastically.

"Exactly. Maybe it's what you need to wake up and see how messed up things are. You need to focus on getting clean and getting her back before some other guy snatches her up."

I rolled over to look at him. "Just thinking about some other guy kissing her or touching her makes me want to fly back to West Virginia and kick his ass."

"Then, you should use that anger to keep your focus. Every time you want to use, picture her with someone else."

"That won't help me. It'll make me lose my mind," I grumbled.

"Just think about it, okay? All that stands between you and Chloe is your powder."

I stayed silent as he turned and left the room. He was insane if he thought his idea would work. Picturing her with someone else would make me go insane. It definitely wouldn't help me stay in control.

I closed my eyes and let the spinning take over until I finally passed out.

Chapter 5

The next few weeks passed by in a blur. We spent most of our time in the studio, recording tracks for the album. Brad seemed satisfied with how fast we were moving, but everyone else's mood was less than happy. The band kept track of me constantly. It was as if they were waiting for me to pass out again. After that one afternoon, I didn't have any more dizzy spells. I always made sure to eat something every morning just in case that was what had caused me to pass out.

The thought of Chloe with someone else was constantly on my mind. I started using more, and I was almost out. I snuck out one night and found a dealer in one of the clubs located in a bad part of L.A. It wasn't hard. While L.A. was an amazing city, there were tons of ghetto areas to choose from.

I tried to keep my addiction under control, but I knew the band was well aware of what I was doing. They tried to talk to me about it occasionally, but I always shut them down before we started fighting. I had no idea what to do. I didn't want to stop, and I wasn't sure if I could. I debated on calling Chloe on more than one occasion, but I stopped myself. She'd probably just hang up on me, and that would make me feel worse.

Brad's voice pulled me away from my thoughts, and I tried to focus on what he was saying.

"You guys did great today. Your single is ready, and I plan on releasing it sometime next week."

We'd spent the entire day working on the album, and I was beat. It was good to know the single would be released soon. At least we weren't doing all of this for nothing. While I knew how much work went into our music, I had no idea how hard it would be to record it professionally. Some days, we would work on just one song, doing it over and over again, until I was sick of it.

"That's awesome! I can't wait to hear us on the radio!" Jade said as she bounced up and down on the balls of her feet.

"Why don't you guys take the rest of the night off? I think we got what we need for today, and you all could use a night to yourselves. Go out and enjoy L.A. nightlife. Pretty soon, you won't be able to without being attacked by fans," Brad said with a smile.

"That's the best thing I've heard all week," Adam said before yawning.

"I'll see you guys in the morning," Brad said.

We told him good-bye and left to enjoy the rest of the night.

After a quick stop at our hotel to shower and change, we took a taxi to West Hollywood where most of the popular clubs were located. We had to stand in line for almost an hour, but we finally managed to get inside one of them. Jade led us to a table in the back, and we all settled in as a waitress appeared to take our orders. I ordered a shot called a cement mixer. I'd heard of it, but I'd never tried it. All I knew was that it was supposed to be strong, and tonight, I needed something strong since Chloe had been on my mind the entire fucking day.

Eric raised an eyebrow at me, but he didn't say anything. Instead, he ordered his beer and sat there with a smirk.

When the waitress returned with our drinks, I laughed when she gave a cute little pink drink to Jade.

"What?" she asked.

"Nothing. I just find it funny that you ordered something girlie instead of your usual beer."

"Oh, shut up and drink your cement." She sipped her drink.

I rolled my eyes as I picked up and then downed my shot. I winced as the taste hit me. It wasn't the best thing I'd ever tasted, but I only cared about the effect. I motioned for the waitress and asked her to bring me another one. Jade and Eric were talking among themselves, and Adam was watching some of the girls on the dance floor.

"I think I need to get laid. It's been too long," Adam said as he sat his beer down and stood up.

I grinned as I watched him maneuver through the swaying bodies. He made his way over to his target—some poor girl sitting at the bar. The girl seemed to like what she saw, and she quickly followed him to the dance floor. Leave it to Adam to score on the first try.

The waitress appeared with my shot, and I downed it quickly. I had snorted a few extra lines before we left, and I was already feeling relaxed. Add some strong alcohol to my system, and I'd be set for the night. I usually had a pretty high tolerance for alcohol, but after a few minutes, I started to feel the beginning of what was sure to be an excellent buzz. Another drink later, and I was set.

I looked up when a pretty blonde in a short red dress approached our table.

She gave me a coy smile as she leaned down. "I'm Carrie. Want to dance?" she whispered in my ear.

She had the same hair color and a name that started with a C. It was as close to Chloe as I was going to get tonight, so I nodded. I followed her to the dance floor and pulled her tight against me as she started to move to the music. My eyes closed as I felt her ass rubbing against my dick. It had been so long since I'd even thought about sex, and this girl was doing everything right.

I spun her around until she was facing me, and I pulled her tight against me. I let my hands roam until they were cupping her ass. Reaching between us, she grabbed my dick through my pants and moaned. Yeah, this girl knew exactly what she was doing. I was hard as a rock as she moved her hand up and down.

"Want to get out of here?" she asked.

"Fuck yeah." I leaned down and kissed her.

She took my hand and led me through the crowd and out a back door. She obviously knew her way around this place. Instead of walking toward the street to hail a taxi, she led me farther down the dark alley. Warning bells might have gone off if everything wasn't so fuzzy in my head. In the dim lighting, she looked just like Chloe. By the time she pushed me up against the wall, I was convinced that she was Chloe.

She unzipped my pants and pushed them down, before sticking her hand inside. When she started stroking me, I moaned.

"God, Chloe. That feels so good."

"I'm not Chloe. I'm Carrie," she said in an irritated voice.

"Mmhmm," I said.

She went to unbutton my shirt. When I felt her tongue flick against one of my nipples, I nearly came in my pants. It had been so long since we'd been together.

"I love you, Chloe, so much."

I almost whimpered when she pulled away.

"I'm *not* Chloe. I'm *Carrie*."

I heard what she said, but her words weren't making sense to me. All I wanted was to bury myself deep inside her.

"Lift your dress, Chloe. I want to bury myself inside you."

"You fucking asshole! I'm *not* Chloe. I suggest you go find her because you're not getting laid by me since you can't even remember my name." She stomped off.

I was left standing in a dark alley with my pants undone and halfway down my legs as I watched her walk away. The fuzziness was getting worse, and I cursed myself for drinking so fast. I wanted to get drunk. I did not want to puke my guts up near some trash.

I fumbled with my pants until I finally pulled them up and fastened them. As I started walking back toward the club, three figures appeared by the door I'd come through earlier. Even drunk, I instantly went on alert as I realized that I was alone and trashed in a damn alley.

"Drake?" a familiar voice asked.

"Jade?"

"We couldn't find you anywhere! Why are you out here?" she asked as they approached me.

"I followed Chloe out here, but she got pissed and left me alone."

"You followed Chloe?" Jade asked in a hesitant voice.

"Yeah, but she left me."

"Did you, uh…did you and Chloe do anything?" she asked.

"No, I told you that she left."

"Oh, thank God. I thought…well, never mind, it doesn't matter. Let's get you back to the hotel, okay?"

I nodded as Eric threw his arm around me to guide me back toward the street. It took both him and Adam to get me into the back of a taxi. I barely realized where I was before they were hauling me out of the taxi and into one of the hotel elevators.

They had some trouble getting me into my room since I had no idea where my key card was. After Jade searched every pocket I had, she finally found it and unlocked the door. They dragged me inside and threw me down onto the bed.

I groaned as I opened my eyes. I could see someone standing over me. "Chloe?"

"No, it's Jade. You're drunk, so get some sleep."

"Chloe, I'm so sorry. I miss you so much. I just want you back. Will you come back to me?"

"He's fucking wasted," Adam said.

"Chloe..." I murmured as I rolled onto my side.

"I can't stand to see him hurting like this. Maybe we should call her," Jade said.

"That won't help anyone. All it will do is freak her out, and you said she's worried as it is. If she knew how bad he was, she'd lose her mind," Eric said.

"Maybe if she saw how much he needed her, she'd come out here to help him," Jade said.

"She won't, and I don't blame her. She's dealt with this kind of thing her entire life. She doesn't deserve to be thrown back into it. Let him sleep it off, and we'll try to get through to him in the morning, not that I think it will do any good," Eric said.

After that, I heard nothing. I felt myself drifting in and out of consciousness for a while until the urge to use the bathroom hit me. I stumbled out of bed and all but crawled to the bathroom. When I was finished, I crawled back to the bed and sat down. I felt like shit, and I needed something to help. I looked out the window and noticed that the sun was already starting to rise. I'd have to be up soon anyway, so I definitely needed a pick-me-up.

I opened the nightstand drawer and pulled out my mirror and bag of cocaine. I knew I'd never make it to the living room, so I laid the mirror down on the bed and dumped the coke out. I tried to make lines the best I could, but I could barely see straight. In a can of soda on the nightstand, I saw a straw, so I grabbed it and used it instead of trying to roll a bill.

When I finished snorting the lines, I threw everything back into the drawer. I glanced at the bag. That was funny. I thought I had more coke than that this morning, but the bag was now empty. I shrugged and then slammed the drawer shut. I draped my body over the bed as I felt it take over.

I must have fallen asleep. The next thing I knew, Jade was standing over me, shaking me, as she screamed at me. I groaned once before I started vomiting.

"He's stable. We've got his fever down, and we've cleared out his lungs. It's a good thing you found him when you did, or he would have suffocated."

"Is he going to be okay?"

"I think so, but we won't know for sure until he wakes up. How long has he been using cocaine?"

"I'm not sure. A couple of months, I think."

"I definitely suggest getting him into some kind of rehabilitation program. The amount of cocaine in his system was astronomical, and if he mixed it with the amount of alcohol you said he drank last night…well, let's just say that he's lucky to be alive."

"We've told him he needs to get help, but he refuses to listen to us. I don't know what to do."

"This isn't going to be easy, but you need to try and convince him when he wakes up. I can keep him here for a few days while his body detoxes, but that's it. Maybe once he detoxes, he will see reason."

"Thank you for everything. I'll try again, but I don't know if he will listen."

I tried to open my eyes to see who was speaking, but I couldn't. On top of that, my entire body felt like a ton of bricks was weighing it down. I finally gave up as unconsciousness took over.

"Any change?"

"He still isn't awake. It's been almost twenty-four hours, Eric. Why isn't he waking up?"

"Don't cry, Jade. Just give him some time."

"I don't know what to do. I'm so scared, and I don't think I can take any more."

"I know. I talked to Brad. He's willing to work with us, but either Drake gets clean, or we're done. Brad said the label would even pay for Drake's treatment if we can get him to go."

"What if he won't? He's refused every time we've tried."

"If he won't, then it's time to walk away. I love him, but I can't keep watching him go through this."

"Jade," I whispered.

"Oh my God! He just said my name."

I heard footsteps approach, but I was out before I had the chance to speak again.

"His eyelids fluttered! Did you see that?"

"I saw it. Hopefully, he'll fully wake up this time."

My body felt like it was on fire. I had no idea where I was. I could hear Adam and Jade's voices. I peeled open my eyes to see them standing above me.

Jade's face broke into a grin as she watched me. "Adam, get Eric and the nurse! He's awake. Drake, can you hear me?"

"Jade?" My throat was burning, and saying her name made me feel like I'd swallowed a sword.

"Yes, it's me. Don't try to talk, okay? Just rest. I'm so glad you're awake. I was so scared."

"Where—" I broke out into a coughing fit that made me want to scream in pain.

"Shh…you're in the hospital. The nurse will explain everything. Just relax."

She took my hand as Adam entered the room with Eric and a young woman following behind him.

"Hey, buddy. It's good to see you awake," Eric said as he approached my bed.

"Good evening, Mr. Allen. I'm Clarissa, your night nurse."

"Water," I managed to croak out.

"Yes, of course." She walked to a nearby table and poured water into a small cup.

When she returned to my bedside, she placed a straw into my mouth, and I started drinking.

"Go slow, or you'll choke," she reprimanded me.

I tried to take smaller sips. When my throat didn't feel like it was on fire, I released the straw, and she set the cup on the table beside me.

"Do you know where you are?" she asked.

I nodded. "Hospital."

"That's right. Do you know why you're here?"

I shook my head. The last thing I remembered was Eric and Adam hauling my drunk ass back to my hotel room.

"You overdosed on cocaine, Mr. Allen. If it wasn't for your friend Jade, you'd be dead right now."

My eyes widened, but I said nothing. How could I have overdosed? I was always careful about how much I used each time. Unless...unless I used while I was drinking. I wanted to smack myself right about now. How could I have been so stupid?

"I'm going to page your doctor. He should be here in just a few minutes."

My eyes moved to Jade as the nurse left. Even though Jade was trying her hardest to hold back her tears, they were slowly sliding down her cheeks.

"Don't...cry," I croaked out. I cursed mentally at my inability to talk. How the hell was I supposed to make things better for her when I couldn't even speak?

"I can't help it. You've been unconscious for over twenty-four hours, and I thought we'd lost you. This has to stop, Drake. I can't take any more."

"So sorry," I whispered.

"I know you are, but that doesn't change anything. You need help. I just hope you can see that now."

I tried to respond, but the doctor decided to walk into the room at that moment.

"Good evening, Mr. Allen. I'm Dr. Brooks, and I've been overseeing your treatment since you were admitted the other morning."

I nodded, not wanting to cause myself any more pain than I had to.

"By now, I'm sure you know you're here because you overdosed on cocaine. I can't stress enough how serious your overdose was. Between the amount of cocaine found in your system and the alcohol you ingested, you are lucky to be alive. If your friends hadn't found you and acted as quickly as they did, you wouldn't be here. You owe them a debt of gratitude."

"How long?" I managed to get out.

"How long have you been here?" he asked.

I nodded. My sense of time was completely screwed-up, and I couldn't even begin to figure out what day it was.

"You were checked in almost two days ago. Your symptoms were vomiting, rapid heart rate, fever, and convulsions. After your friends told me that you were an addict, we were able to treat you quickly enough to prevent any long-term effects."

"Thank you."

"You're very welcome, Mr. Allen. I sincerely hope that this will serve as a much needed wake-up call. You should not mess around with cocaine, and you obviously need help. I want to keep you here for a few more days just to make sure you have no other issues. I suggest you take this time to consider your treatment options. Now that you're conscious, you will feel the withdrawal side effects from not using cocaine for a couple of days. Our staff can help you deal with them as you detox. After that, I suggest you check yourself into a rehabilitation center."

Before waking up in the hospital like this, I would have refused. I wasn't so sure now. I always felt like I had everything under control, but that was obviously a huge misconception on my part.

"I'll leave you alone with your friends now. I'm sure they have a lot they'd like to say to you."

He exchanged a look with my band mates before he left. They had obviously had discussions about me while I was unconscious.

Eric approached my bed and sat down in the chair beside me. "How are you feeling?"

"Like shit."

He smiled at me, but there was no humor in his eyes. "I would assume so. You scared the shit out of us, Drake. We thought you were dead."

"Sorry."

"We know you are, but like Jade said, it doesn't change anything. We've been talking about your situation, and Brad has also put in his two cents. Here's the deal—either you get help, or our contract with the label is gone. As much as I hate to do it, you will no longer be a part of the band. We're not doing this because we're assholes. We're doing it because we care."

This was it. I was going to lose everything. I'd already lost Chloe, and now, I was losing my friends and my career, too.

Jade grabbed my hand and held it in hers. "Don't try to talk right now. Just think about it. We can't force you to get help, but we're asking as your friends and your band members. I love you, but I can't stand to watch you self-destruct any longer."

"I'm with them. You're not our Drake anymore," Adam added as he sat down in the chair across the room from us. "I'm not going to get all mushy and tell you how much I love you, but you know you're like a brother to me. You need help, bro."

"I know," I whispered.

"Good. We'll leave you alone to think about things while we go grab some dinner. We'll be back soon, okay?" Jade said.

I nodded, and they walked out of the room. When I was finally alone, everything hit me at once. In the last few months, I'd destroyed every relationship that I cared about. I'd pushed Chloe away first and then the band. Besides my uncle, they were the only family I had. I wasn't ready to give them up, but I wasn't sure I could stop using either. If I couldn't, I'd lose everything. Surely, that would be enough motivation to keep me going, wouldn't it? I wasn't ready to face my demons, but I had to try.

As I lay there, fighting with myself, the nurse walked into the room with a tray.

"I brought you some soup. I'm sure your throat is raw from the breathing tube we had to put in during the first few hours you were here, but this should help." She set the tray on a cart and pulled it over to me.

I felt like an invalid as she helped me sit up. My hands were shaking as I picked up my spoon and dipped it into the soup in front of me. I cursed to myself when I dropped the spoon and had to start over. My muscles felt weak, and I wasn't sure I could even bring the spoon up to my mouth. After a few tries, I finally managed it. The soup hurt like hell as it went down, but I kept eating anyway. The nurse had to help me after a while, and I wanted to scream. I couldn't even lift a damn spoon. I'd really fucked myself up this time.

"Don't get discouraged. Your body is starting the withdrawal process, so shaking and muscle weakness is normal. It's going to be rough for the next few days, but if you can make it through, you will be just fine."

I nodded as she continued to spoon-feed me.

"I know it seems impossible right now, but you can beat this, Mr. Allen. Your friends have told me all about you, and it sounds like you are a strong-willed individual. You can do this." She picked up the tray with the now empty bowl on it.

I wasn't sure why she was giving me a pep talk, but I appreciated it.

Jade and the guys came back a couple of hours later. I gave them a weak smile as they sat down around me.

"Hey," I said in a clear voice. The soup had really helped my throat. At least it didn't feel like I'd eaten a sword when I talked now.

"Did you think things over?" Jade asked, getting right to the point.

I nodded. "I did."

"And?" Eric asked.

"I need help." It almost killed me to admit that, but I knew it was true. There was nothing like waking up in a hospital to knock some sense into me.

"Finally!" Jade shouted as she threw herself at me.

I couldn't help but laugh as she held me in a death grip.

Eric smiled at me. "I'm glad to hear it. We'll be with you the whole way."

"It's about damn time." Adam muttered.

I looked at all three of them and prayed that I would be strong enough to do this. I needed help, and I was going to get it.

Chapter

Over the next few days, I learned exactly what hell felt like. Now that I was conscious, my body demanded that I find my next fix. It took every ounce of willpower I possessed to hold myself back from running out of the hospital to go to my hotel room where my stash was waiting for me. It was quite possibly the cruelest punishment I had ever known.

My body was going nuts, trying to deal with the fact that it was no longer getting its needed daily dose of cocaine. Even though the nurses had tried to prepare me, I was knocked on my ass by the muscle spasms, nausea, vomiting, and all the other things that came with withdrawal. I felt like I had the flu, but this particular flu had decided to take steroids and beef up a bit.

Over the next couple days, the physical symptoms were still horrible, but the mental side of things became almost unbearable. I was at war with myself. Part of me was fighting this with everything it had, but the other part was on its knees, begging and pleading with me to cave. All of the feelings—the guilt, the anger, the pain—that I'd suppressed with the cocaine were coming to the surface. I couldn't help but be depressed. Without the cocaine to make me feel like everything was going to be okay, I realized just how fucked-up my life was.

I lashed out at everyone around me—the band, the nurses, and even my doctor. I hated all of them for pushing me to stop, and I made sure that they knew it. I expected the band to get sick of me and leave, but instead, they stayed by my side constantly. At times, I appreciated it, but most of the time, I just wanted them to go away. It was hard to wallow in self-pity when I had three assholes always trying to cheer me up.

On my last day in the hospital, my symptoms were finally starting to fade. The relief I felt could not be described with words. Even though the depression seemed to stick with me, I started to feel like my old self more and more. I was convinced that I could stay away from the drugs without checking into rehab, but when I mentioned it to the others, they refused to believe me.

After several arguments, I finally gave in and agreed to check right into a rehab program.

As I walked up the steps to the facility that would be my home for the next few months, I felt hopelessness begin to take over. I didn't want to be in this prison. The building itself was beautiful, but looks were often deceiving. It appeared to be too cheery and bright to be a place where so many people suffered every day.

My friends and I walked in and approached the reception desk in the lobby.

A young woman looked up and smiled. "Hi, can I help you?"

Jade gave me a small shove, forcing me to the front of our group.

I turned and glared at her before I faced the receptionist again. "I'm Drake Allen. I'm supposed to check in today."

"Of course!" She picked up a clipboard and handed it to me. "Please fill out these forms for me, and then we can get the ball rolling. Just bring them back to me when you're finished."

I walked over to several empty chairs. I sat down and started filling out the forms, and the band followed and took seats around me. The beginning was mostly standard information—name, address, phone number—but the following pages focused on questions that I wasn't ready to answer. My addiction was my problem, and I didn't want to spill my guts to strangers. I answered the majority of the questions and then returned the clipboard to the receptionist.

"Have a seat, and I will let one of the nurses know you're here," she said as she took the clipboard from me.

I walked back to my seat, sat down, and started tapping my foot. I didn't want to sit. I wanted to walk out of this fucking place and never look back. But I couldn't. If I did, the band would drop me, and we would lose our one chance at making it big in the recording world. Plus, I wanted Chloe back. I needed to be sure that I could stay clean before I made any attempts to win her over.

I looked up when the door beside the reception desk opened. A pretty young nurse stepped out and looked around. As soon as she saw our group, she started walking in our direction. I forced myself to sit still, instead of running for the exit like I wanted to. I had to do this.

She stopped in front of me and looked at Eric, Adam, and me. "Drake Allen?"

Adam pointed at me. "That would be him. Take him away."

I turned to glare at Adam. I didn't need a babysitter, and I sure as hell could tell the nurse my name.

"Follow me, please," she said, looking at me.

"Can they come with me?" I asked as I stood from my seat. Even if it made me weak to admit it, I wasn't sure I could do this on my own.

She gave me a sympathetic look. "I'm sorry, but they can't. They can come back on Sunday. That's our visitation day."

I froze. There was no way I could do this if they weren't around me. My friends and Chloe were the only reasons I was doing this, and without them, it was hopeless.

Jade stepped in front of me and gripped my face with both of her hands. "Look at me. It will be fine. You can do this without us hanging around all the time. You're such a strong person, Drake."

"I don't know if I can," I whispered so that only she could hear.

"Well, I do. We will be here every Sunday to hang out, so just focus on that when it gets hard. We love you."

I pulled her into a hug. "I love you, too. You might as well be my sister."

She pulled away and smiled at me. "As far as I'm concerned, I am your sister. Now, go kick ass."

I kissed her on the forehead before following the nurse through a door and down a hallway to an exam room. She checked my vitals and recorded everything before having me step on the scale.

She frowned when she wrote the number in my chart. "Are you sure about the weight you put down in the questionnaire?"

"I guess. It's been a couple of months since I weighed myself." Checking the scale wasn't exactly one of my top priorities. I wasn't some chick who freaked out about her weight.

"Based on your weight noted here and what the scale says, you've lost almost twenty pounds."

I shrugged. "We've been on the road a lot. Eating wasn't exactly my top concern."

She pursed her lips and said nothing more.

I rolled my eyes, annoyed with her. So what if I'd lost weight? It wasn't like it mattered. I wasn't in here for an eating disorder. I'd snorted cocaine. Focus here, woman.

"Follow me, please." She opened the door and walked back into the hallway.

I followed silently behind her as we made our way down the hall. She stopped in front of a door with the name *Dr. Peters* written on it. She knocked softly before swinging the door open and stepping back to let me pass by. I walked in and looked around. The office was nice. There wasn't much in the decorations department, and the room was crammed full of filing cabinets. A large wooden desk sat in the center with a few chairs surrounding it.

A man, Dr. Peters I assumed, was sitting behind the desk. He looked up and smiled as we entered. He was older, probably in his late fifties, with a large bald spot and several lines etched onto his face.

"Hi, Lisa. What can I help you with?" he asked.

"This is Drake Allen, our newest patient." The nurse walked to his desk and handed him my file.

"Thank you, Lisa." Still in his seat, he leaned forward toward me and extended his hand. "Hi, Drake. I'm Dr. Peters. It's good to meet you."

I was surprised by his strong Southern accent. I didn't think it was common out here in California.

I stepped forward and shook his hand. This guy was my ticket to getting out of here, so I figured it would be a good idea to get on his good side. "Likewise."

He glanced up at the nurse. "I can take it from here, Lisa. Thank you for checking him in."

"Of course. If you need anything else, just call the front desk," Lisa said before walking out the door.

"All right, Drake. If you don't mind waiting for a few minutes, I'd like to go over your file really quick."

"Sure." I sat down across from him.

I waited patiently as he flipped through the pages in the file.

After a few minutes, he put my file on the desk and looked up at me. "Well, now that I've read who you are on paper, why don't you tell me in your own words what's been going on with you?"

I raised an eyebrow. "Uh, sorry? I'm not sure what you're asking."

"I can sit here and read your file all day, but when it comes right down to it, I don't give a shit what's in this file. I want to hear from you about where you're at in your life."

"Did you just say *shit*?" I asked, shocked.

"I did. Don't act so surprised. I'm sure you've heard worse."

"But...you're a doctor. Isn't there some kind of code that says you have to be an uptight asshole?"

He laughed. "I think I'm going to like you, Drake. And no, there's no code against my vocabulary. You might as well get used to it."

I had to admit that I liked this guy. I wasn't sure if this was his way of getting into my head or what, but it was working. I had expected to work with some doctor who had a stick shoved up his ass.

"So, tell me what's been happening. I know you're here to get treatment for your cocaine addiction, and that's a hard thing to do."

"What do you want to know?" I asked.

"Everything. Why did you start? Why do you want to stop? What is your favorite food?"

I laughed. "Pop Tarts on that last one. The rest isn't so simple."

"I've got time."

I sighed as I ran my hands through my hair. I sucked at this sharing stuff. He seemed like a cool guy, but I didn't want to sit around a campfire with him, singing "Kumbaya" and talking about my feelings.

"I don't know why I started. I guess I used it to escape something that happened."

"And what was that something?"

"I thought my girlfriend was cheating on me. It turned out that I had been wrong, but I couldn't seem to stop after that. Then, other things happened, and I started using more. I thought I had it under control but apparently not. Now, I'm here, so you can fix me."

"I can't fix you, Drake. Only you can do that, but I am here to help you. I want you to start from the beginning and tell me everything that has happened since you thought your girlfriend was cheating on you."

I opened my mouth and did what he'd asked. I started with the pictures Kadi had given me and went from there. I discussed everything that had happened with Logan, Jordan, and Chloe's mother's death. When I got to the part about Chloe leaving me, I had to stop for a moment. It hurt too much to think about what I'd lost.

When I finished, I felt like a weight had been lifted off my chest. I always kept everything trapped inside, and it felt nice to put all my cards on the table for someone else to deal with.

"It sounds like you've been through a lot over the last few months. I saw in your file that you were enrolled in a program similar to this when you were younger. Knowing that you've abused drugs before, I can understand why it was so simple for you to fall back into them. Those who have used drugs often consider them a safe haven."

"Yeah, that's a good way to put it—a safe haven. It felt like no one could touch me when I used them."

"Exactly. Obviously, you know better now, or you wouldn't be sitting in my office. The physician who treated you at the hospital had your file sent over earlier today, and I skimmed through it. I have to say that you're very lucky to be alive. The amount of cocaine in your system was excessively high. When mixed with alcohol, it makes what I like to call, the undertaker's cocktail. Before we move any further, I need you to give me an honest answer to a difficult question. Did you do that to yourself on purpose?"

I'd been staring at the carpet, but my head snapped up at his words. "You think I tried to kill myself?"

"If you did, there's no need to feel ashamed. You haven't had the best of luck these past few months. Combining that with cocaine could lead to suicidal thoughts."

I held up my hand. "Let's just stop right there. I would not kill myself, no matter how bad things got. Am I depressed? Sure. But that doesn't mean I'm going to go off myself."

"That's good to hear. Don't take offense to my questions. I'm simply trying to get to know you better."

"None taken."

He nodded. "Good. So, anyway, back on the matter at hand. While in the hospital, you agreed to go into this program. Why?"

"I didn't have any other options. If I didn't do this, then the band and the label said they would drop me. I was forced to be here."

"No one can force you to do anything, Drake. You need to make the decision on your own, or nothing I do will benefit you. I can sit here and preach to you all day, but until you realize that you need help, nothing I say will matter."

"I don't need help. I've been clean for over a week. I told them that I could do this on my own, but they refused to listen."

"Being clean and staying clean are two totally different things. While you might feel like you can handle your addiction now, what will you do when things get tough? Cocaine was your coping mechanism, and you will feel the need to use it again. What I'm here for is to help you come to terms with your addiction and to help you learn to deal with things in a healthier way."

I nodded, unsure of what to say. I understood where he was coming from, but I didn't think that I would relapse. The hell that I had just gone through in the hospital was enough to scare me away from it for a long time.

But what if he was right? What if I contacted Chloe, and she didn't want anything to do with me even if I was clean? I didn't know if I could handle that. Life was always so fucking hard, and I'd refused to deal with it. I always found a way to make me forget—drugs, women, and finally Chloe. I didn't accept anything. I evaded.

"I think we've chatted enough for one day. I will have one of the nurses take you to your room, so you can get settled in. I want to meet with you tomorrow to start our sessions. Does that sound good to you?" Dr. Peters asked as he smiled at me.

"Do I have a choice?" I asked, sarcasm filling my voice.

He smiled. "You always have a choice, Drake."

After a nurse took me to my room, I spent the rest of the evening unpacking the bag Jade had left for me at the front desk. It had pissed me off that I hadn't been allowed to bring it to my room myself, but of course, the nurses had to search it before I could have it back. The band had known that I had hidden cocaine in my hotel room previously, and they had refused to let me pack my belongings by myself just in case I had more hidden, so they'd done it for me. I'd felt highly annoyed with them, but I'd let it go. It had been one of those pick-your-battles kind of moments.

The nurse had taken my cell phone with her when she left, much to my annoyance. According to her, it was a policy to take all cell phones from patients when they entered the program. She said something about not letting the outside world affect me while I was in the process of getting better. It might be policy, but that didn't mean I was happy about it.

I hated that I felt truly here, but I was more concerned about the fact that I couldn't contact Chloe. Even though I hadn't contacted her in months, I still had her number in my cell. There had been so many times when I'd picked it up to call her, only to throw the phone. Now, it felt like any connection I had with her, no matter how small, was gone. I wished that she were here. I always felt like a loose cannon when she wasn't around. There was just something about her that always calmed me.

The nurse had given me a sheet of paper that listed all the center's rules. I quickly read through it. Most of them were simple—no drugs, no fighting, and other things like that. The only positive part of the entire day was that I was allowed to smoke, and I headed outside to do just that. If they'd also taken smoking away from me, I wasn't sure I would last in here. I couldn't give up all my nasty habits at once.

Everything around here was on a schedule. Along with specific times for meals and recreational activities, I had a specific time that I would meet with Dr. Peters each day. I was surprised that I wasn't given a bathroom schedule, too. Due to my connection with the label, Brad exerted a lot of pressure, and I was excused from group therapy sessions. The label didn't want it getting out to the press and our fans that I was in here. It would be bad for business.

I headed back inside and returned to my room. After settling in for the night, I tossed and turned for over an hour before I finally passed out.

Chapter 7

"It's good to see you again, Drake. Please close the door behind you and have a seat," Dr. Peters said.

I stepped inside his office and did as he'd said. I sat down in the chair across from him.

"I hope your first night here was pleasant."

"It was fine. Thank you." In all honesty, I had expected to hear people screaming throughout the night, like I had seen in movies, but the place had been completely silent. Maybe they really didn't torture people to death in here.

"Glad to hear it. Now, let's get down to business."

Or maybe they did torture us.

"Sure. Why not?"

He smiled at me. "I promise you that this will be a lot easier if you cooperate with me. Instead of thinking of this as a punishment, consider it a surprise vacation. Maybe that will help you to accept it better."

"Bring on the drinks and the beach," I grumbled.

I was extra cranky this morning, and unfortunately for Dr. Peters, he was getting the shit end of the deal. I didn't want to be here, and I had no intentions of spilling my guts like I had yesterday.

"That's the spirit!" He laughed. Apparently, he wasn't familiar with sarcasm. "Yesterday, we skimmed over the last few months. Today, I want to go back a bit further. We mentioned a prior drug issue, and I'd like to go over it."

Great. I would be spending the day talking about my dead parents and my stupidity during my high school years. Just throw me off the damn building, and put me out of my misery.

"Yippee."

"I know this is hard for you, Drake, but you need to open up to me, so we can figure out why you keep turning to drugs. Can you tell me why you started using them when you were younger?" Dr. Peters asked.

"I was just a kid and bored most of the time. My friends did them, so I did, too. I'm just a good example of peer pressure."

"I guess so. Can you tell me about your home life back then? Did you fight with your parents a lot?"

"Nope. My parents died when I was ten, so I lived with my uncle."

"I'm sorry to hear that, Drake. I didn't see that in your file. I know it's hard to deal with losing a parent, especially both. What happened to them?"

"Some asshole was drunk and hit them."

"I see. I'm sure it was a terrible time for both you and your uncle."

"It was for me. I'm not sure how he felt. He was in the military, so he worked a lot. We never really talked about their deaths. He took me in, but he left me alone to do my own thing."

"How long has it been since you've spoken with your uncle?"

I shrugged. "It's been a while. I think it was a few months before Chloe and I got together. He's currently deployed again."

"So, it's safe to say that you're not close with your uncle?"

"I guess. I mean, I like him and all, but we never really clicked. I owe him a lot though. He took me in when I had no one else, and he forced me into rehab last time."

"It sounds like he cares a lot about you, but he just doesn't show it that often. Did that ever bother you?"

"Not really. He could never replace my parents, and I never expected him to. I've been on my own for most of my life, and I like it that way."

Dr. Peters nodded. "I see."

We sat in silence, both of us staring at each other. I wasn't sure if he was waiting for me to continue telling him about my childhood or what. If he was, he was out of luck. I thought I was going to explode from the silence in the room.

Then, he finally spoke. "Tell me about your drug habits as a teenager."

"Why does it matter? It was a long time ago." I was suddenly annoyed with him.

"I'm just trying to get a better feel for you, Drake. While the past is the past, it often affects our decisions later on in life."

I started to roll my eyes, but I caught myself at the last minute. "There isn't much to tell. I was left at home, unsupervised a lot, and I started smoking weed with my friends. When we were old enough to go to the cool parties, I began using any drugs that were available to me. I mainly took pills, but I used acid and cocaine from time to time."

"And how did you handle rehab when your uncle forced you into going?" he asked as he wrote something in my chart.

"Like any sixteen-year-old would. I was pissed, and I fought it for a while. When I finally managed to straighten up, they released me."

"So, you've always been stubborn?" He grinned at me.

I couldn't help but laugh. "Yeah, I guess so."

"It's not a bad thing to be stubborn, you know. It just means you know what you want out of life."

"I guess so. I never really thought about it like that. When people tell me I'm stubborn, it's usually intended as an insult."

"That was not how I intended for it to be interpreted. Anyway, how did you handle things after you were released from rehab?"

"I was okay. I met up with Jade and the guys right after, and we started our band, Breaking the Hunger. I used it as a distraction when things sucked in my life. Plus, I was sixteen and in a band. Do you have any idea how many girls there were to distract me? I mean, come on, it's every sixteen-year-old boy's fantasy to have older girls throwing themselves at you!"

He laughed. "I'm sure it was quite entertaining for you and I'm also sure you had several girlfriends during that time."

"No way. There was no way I was going to tie myself to one girl when I could have them all."

Wow, I sounded like a complete douche canoe, but it was true. I'd spent the last few years with more women than I could count. It wasn't my fault they were all sluts and threw themselves at me.

He raised an eyebrow at my statement. "Exactly how often were you with different women, Drake?"

"Once the band started getting popular, I was usually with a different one every night."

"That's quite a lot. Did it ever bother you that you slept with so many different women?"

"Not really. I guess I used them instead of drugs. If I was pissed off or down, I'd just take one of them back to my uncle's house. The band lied and told the bars that I was eighteen, so we could play in them. I don't think any of the women realized just how young I was. They might have felt bad if they did, but I doubt it. Women like that are only after one thing, and I was glad to help them."

Yeah, I was definitely getting the asshole-of-the-year award after this conversation. Sure, after I got with Chloe, I'd regretted sleeping with so many women, but I'd never thought about how screwed-up I was to do it.

"Wow, I'm an asshole, aren't I?" I asked.

"I don't think you're an asshole per se. I think you just used those women to deal with things. How long did this go on for?"

"Until a few months before Chloe and I got together. After I realized how I felt about her, I still slept with various women for a while. I knew it was wrong, but I couldn't seem to stop. Then, I was watching Chloe in class one day, and I realized I could do a hell of a lot better. She saw the good in me even though I couldn't see it in myself. I love her so much."

"And she left you when she discovered your habit?" he asked.

"Yeah, she said she couldn't be around someone like me again. Her mother was always high, and she had abused Chloe throughout her entire life. I guess she was afraid that I'd do the same thing."

"And would you?"

"Of course not! I love her! I would never hit her!"

"There are different kinds of abuse, Drake. It's not just physical. There are mental aspects as well."

"I admit that I got angry a lot, but I don't think I abused her in any way. She left before things turned bad."

"You said that you still love her. Do you think there is hope for the two of you?"

That was the million-dollar question. I was hoping that she would take me back, but there were no guarantees. She might have moved on by now anyway.

"I don't know. I hope so though. I fucked up the only relationship I ever cared about. I feel like I can't breathe without her around."

"I'm simply making an observation here, but I think that you are the type of person who requires a coping mechanism at all times. First, you used drugs, then women, then Chloe, and finally, you went back to drugs. Why do you think that is?"

"The drugs and women served as a distraction, but Chloe was different. She made me feel things I didn't think I could ever feel. She made me feel like I was alive for the first time in my life."

"I think we've figured out where things went wrong with you. You never deal with any of your problems. You simply push them to the side and use drugs and sex to distract yourself. If we can teach you how to face things head-on, I think you will be able to go through life without the fear of a relapse."

I grinned. "You've already figured me out, doc…and with only two sessions. I'm impressed. If you keep it up, I'll be out of here by next week."

He laughed. "I wouldn't go that far. We have a lot of work to do, but I have faith in you. You can beat this." He glanced down at his watch. "I think that's enough for one day. I'll see you tomorrow."

I stood up before he even finished speaking. "Works for me."

"I want you to think about what we discussed today. Remember, you are in control of how long this process takes. The sooner you can come to terms with everything, the faster you will be out of here."

During the rest of the week, our sessions were much like the first one. We would always go over everything from the session before, and then we'd move on to new topics. I had to admit that Dr. Peters seemed to know what he was doing. Every time I walked into his office, my need to hold back faded. As much as I hated to admit it, talking to him helped me, and I was learning a lot about myself.

I wouldn't deal with my problems. Instead, I'd run away. At the first sign of trouble, I'd run to the nearest distraction, and I'd hide until the storm passed. This last time though, I'd used cocaine when I felt the storm coming back. Without it in my system, I was forced to deal with my actions over the last few months. There were things that I regretted so much—especially my jealously with Chloe and Jordan's friendship and my anger toward her. She didn't deserve the way I had treated her.

My first visitation was on Sunday. Jade, Eric, and Adam came, just like they had said they would. It felt strange at first. We weren't sure what to say to each other. But after a few minutes of forced conversation, I finally opened my mouth and apologized for being such a dick for so long. After that, some of the tension eased, and it seemed like old times, like we were back in West Virginia, talking and joking in my kitchen or at the bar. When it was time to go, Jade hugged me tightly. "I'm so proud of you. I can already see such a big change in you already."

Over the next few weeks, I learned to deal with my demons. Dr. Peters started at the very beginning with the deaths of my parents. I realized that I'd never really accepted their deaths even though I thought that I had long ago. During that session, I broke down and cried for the first time in years. I missed them so damn much. How was it fair that they had been taken from me when I was only fucking ten years old? What had I ever done to deserve that?

When I asked Dr. Peters that, he frowned. "No one ever deserves something like that. This world is a hard place to live in, and you were forced to learn that at an early age. No one blames you for feeling angry or betrayed. Anyone in your position would feel the same way."

"Will I ever really be able to move on?"

"You will, but it'll take time. You've spent so much of your life running from it that you never truly took the time to mourn them. You accepted their deaths the first time you were sent to a rehabilitation program, but you never dealt with it."

Well, I was definitely mourning them now. It felt like my heart was being ripped out as I let myself finally feel the pain of their deaths. I let the pain overtake me until I was paralyzed with it. I wanted to escape from it, but I didn't. Dr. Peters was right. I always ran, and right now, I was tired of running. It was time to face my demons and start over.

After learning to deal with my parents' deaths, I was almost glad when we moved on to Chloe. I was learning to look at things differently, and compared to my parents, talking about Chloe was easy. While I knew that I'd lost her, I still had hope that I could have her back in my life again. Dr. Peters explained that while it was important to depend on my significant other, it was unhealthy to feel like I couldn't live without her. I loved Chloe, but I also needed her in an unhealthy way.

He worked with me to help separate the two sides of my relationship with her, love and need, and in doing so, I realized that he was right. I'd depended on her in a way that I shouldn't have. My feelings for her never changed, but I realized that I'd put her on a pedestal as my saving angel when I didn't need to.

Through all of this, I felt myself growing stronger, both mentally and physically. Now that I was actually eating at least three times a day, I was gaining back all of the weight that I'd lost from using cocaine. I spent most of my recreational time outside, and my pale skin was starting to bronze. Between the weight gain and free tanning, I was starting to look human again. When I first entered the program, I'd thought that I looked fine. The first night that I came here, the nurse had snapped a picture for my identification card. When I looked at it weeks later, I was shocked. I'd looked horrible. My skin had been pasty, my eyes had appeared dead, and I'd looked almost skeletal compared to how I looked now. It was amazing how much I'd changed since I came here. I felt like a new person.

As my time in the program came to a close, I had to admit that I was relieved. Now that I was able to see things clearly, I wanted to get back out into the real world and start living my life again. I wanted to fix things with the band first, and then it would be time to find Chloe. I had already mentally prepared myself for the possibility that she might not want me back, but I wouldn't let go of my last string of hope. I loved her more than ever now, and I wanted to prove it to her.

When I walked into Dr. Peters's office to say good-bye, it just felt right. I was ready to move on with my life.

He glanced up at me. "Hello, Drake. I assume this is your farewell visit."

"It is. I just wanted to say good-bye and thank you for everything."

"No thanks are needed. You did all the work. I was just here to help you along."

"Well, you did your job then. I haven't felt this good in a long time."

"I'm glad to hear it. If you ever need anything, you have my number. Don't hesitate to call me, and I mean that." He pulled a piece of paper out of his desk drawer. "And here is your certificate for completing the program. I thought you might need it as proof for certain people."

Chloe. He knew that I was going to go after her, and he wanted to help me in any way he could.

"I will, and thanks again, doc." I waved and then turned to walk out the door.

As soon as I reached the desk in the main lobby, I heard someone shouting my name. I looked up just in time to see Jade throwing herself at me. She wrapped her arms around me and buried her face in my neck.

"Whoa! Hi to you, too." I pried her off of me.

"Sorry. I'm just so excited. You're free!"

Eric and Adam were standing a few feet away. Both of them were grinning from ear to ear.

Eric stepped closer and gave me one of those one-armed hugs that only guys could pull off. "It's good to have you back."

"It's good to be back. I'm ready to get out of here."

I glanced at Adam, but he rolled his eyes. "Don't expect me to get all misty eyed over you. I'm glad you're back. Let's leave it at that."

I laughed. "Missed you, too, jackass."

It took me a few minutes to sign all the paperwork to check myself out. As soon as I was finished, I followed the band out to the parking lot. They stopped in front of a brand-new Dodge Charger.

"Who does this belong to?" I asked.

"That would be me. It was the first thing I bought with the money from the label," Adam said as he unlocked the car.

"He's not kidding either. As soon as they put the money into our accounts, he went to the dealership and bought this thing." Jade said as she shook her head.

"I hope it lasts longer than the rest of your cars." I grinned.

"Fuck off and get in," Adam growled. "And don't scratch my baby." He sat down in the driver's seat.

Jade took the passenger seat while Eric and I climbed into the back. I had to admit that Adam's new car was a sweet ride, but I still preferred my baby back home. Hopefully, I could go back and pick it up soon.

Jade turned around to look at me. "We just signed the papers for your new place yesterday. Are you ready to see it?"

On their last visit, she had informed me that they were going to get me a place, so I'd have somewhere to go once I was released.

"Yeah, but I need to make one stop first," I said.

"Sure. Where to?" Adam asked as he started the car. He began pulling out of the lot.

"The nearest jewelry store."

Chapter

I couldn't remember the last time that I'd been this nervous. I could do this. I knew I could. Then, why had I sat in my car for the last hour, staring at the house across the street from me? I needed to man up and take care of this shit.

It had taken me forever to find her. Without thinking, I'd driven to the dorm where she was staying before she moved in with me. I walked straight up to her room and knocked on the door. Imagine my surprise when two girls who I'd never seen before had answered the door. I'd tried Amber's room next, but again, two girls who I didn't know had greeted me. I'd even tried the bar, hoping that maybe she still came in here occasionally. No one had seen her in months. It was like she'd just disappeared from the face of the Earth. When I'd stopped at her Starbucks, at least people knew who she was, but they had no idea where she could be. She hadn't worked there since we left the summer before.

I'd finally hit some luck when I stopped at a gas station to fill-up.

Her old roommate, Rachel, pulled in next to me. When she got out of her car, the shocked look on her face was priceless. I knew it was safe to say that Rachel had talked to her since our split. There was no other explanation for the way her mouth had dropped open.

"Hey, Rachel."

"Drake? Holy crap, it is you! What are you doing back here?"

"Trying to find Chloe. The keyword there is trying. Do you know where she is?"

She bit her lip, clearly debating on whether or not to tell me.

"Please. I need to find her," I pleaded.

"I'll tell you where she is, but if this goes south, don't tell her it was me."

I grabbed a crumpled piece of paper and a pen out of my car. I smoothed out the paper, and I wrote down the directions as she gave them to me.

I started to get into my car, but then I stopped. "Rachel?"

She looked up. "Yeah?"

"Is she...I mean...is Chloe with anyone?"

She gave me a small smile. "Not that I know of."

I wanted to jump up and down, scream, and fist-pump, but I contained myself. Chloe wasn't with anyone. She hadn't forgotten about me.

"Thank you."

I pulled myself back to the present as I threw open my door and walked across the street to her house. If I didn't do this now, I never would. Before I chickened out, I pounded on the door. I waited a minute or two before knocking again. There were lights on inside, so I knew someone had to be home. If no one would answer, I planned on sitting in my car until someone opened the door.

Just as I was turning to walk away, the door flew open.

"Yes?" Chloe asked grumpily.

I turned to face her and froze for a second. She was as beautiful as I remembered. She had her hair tied back in a messy bun and was in old sweatpants and a simple shirt, but she still took my breath away. It had been like this from the beginning. There was just something about this woman.

"Hi, Chloe." I gave her a small smile.

Her eyes widened in shock just before she slammed the door in my face. Well, that went as I'd expected, but I wasn't about to give up that easily. The girl was going to talk to me whether she wanted to or not. I stepped forward and pushed the doorbell that I hadn't noticed before.

I could hear someone shouting inside, and then it was absolutely quiet. Now, what the hell was I supposed to do? Should I stand on her porch all night and hope that she came out eventually?

My head snapped up as the front door opened again. Instead of seeing Chloe, Amber stepped outside and closed the door quietly.

"Well, if it isn't Mr. Rock Star himself," she growled.

It was safe to say that Amber wasn't a fan of mine.

"Hi, Amber. How have you been?"

"Don't even. Chloe hasn't heard from you in months, and then you just show up on our doorstep with no warning! You are the biggest asshole on the planet, Drake Allen!"

"I know I am, okay? You have every right to be mad at me, but I need to talk to Chloe."

"Why? What could you possibly have to say to her that will fix the past six months of her life? You destroyed her, Drake! Just when I thought she was doing better, you come back and fuck it up all over again. She's trying to move on!"

"I don't want her to move on, Amber. I love her, and I can't stand the thought of her being with someone else."

"Then, why didn't you come back before now? You broke her, and Logan and I were left to pick up the pieces!"

"I couldn't." I ignored the jealousy I felt about Logan taking care of Chloe.

"Couldn't? Or didn't want to?" She glared at me.

"I couldn't. I wanted to come after her, but I knew she'd never give me the time of day until I got my shit together."

"And have you? Or are you still using?"

"I'm clean. I went into rehab and sobered up. I spent the last month making sure I could do it, and now, I'm back for what's mine. I love her, Amber, and I can't give up on us until I see her one last time. If she doesn't want me anymore, then so be it, but I have to try."

116

Amber looked at me. I knew she was trying to figure out if I was telling the truth. "You two were perfect together. I've never seen her as happy as she was with you."

"Until I fucked it all up," I said, ashamed to admit the truth.

"Until you fucked everything up. I've always liked you, Drake. Really, I have. But I don't want to see her go through what she's went through these last few months again."

"I'll never hurt her again. Please let me talk to her. I just want to explain everything. I want to spend the rest of my life with her."

She raised an eyebrow. "You do realize that you're a rock star now? At least, you're almost one. You'll have thousands of women throwing themselves at you. Do you really think you'll be able to be faithful to Chloe?"

"I couldn't care less about any other woman out there. Chloe is the only girl I've ever cared about."

She sighed. "I'll help you, but this doesn't mean that I don't think you're an asshole. Because I do."

I smiled. "I'll make it up to you, too. I swear. I'm sure you'd like to see Adam sometime soon."

Amber's cheeks turned bright red, but she pretended not to be bothered by my mention of my band mate.

"I couldn't care less about Adam. Now, come on, I'll sneak you inside."

She stepped back into the house, looked around, and then motioned for me to follow. She led me into the living room and pointed to a chair. "Sit there and be quiet. I'll see if I can get Chloe to come out of her room."

I watched as she turned and disappeared down the hallway. I heard her open a door and close it. Then, the house was eerily silent, and I strained my ears to hear anything else. After a few minutes, I finally gave up and slouched down into the chair. I was going to get my chance to talk to Chloe, and I didn't want to mess it up. This was my one shot, my only shot, to prove to her that she mattered to me. No pressure or anything.

Finally, a door opened, and then I heard Amber and Chloe talking as they came down the hallway. This was it—now or never.

Amber and Chloe appeared a second later. Chloe didn't even glance my way as she walked to the couch and sat down. Amber, on the other hand, stopped right in front of me, trying to block Chloe from seeing me.

"Thanks for being here for me, Amber. I don't think I would have made it through these last few months without you," Chloe said as she pressed the play button on the remote.

"Uh, no problem. Listen—" Amber started to say.

Chloe interrupted her. "I'm serious. We both know I was a fucking wreck, and you helped me get my shit together. If there's one thing I've learned from all of this, it's that men are total and complete dicks."

"Well, see, Chloe—" Amber said, trying to get her to shut up.

"Take my word for it. Men are nothing but coldhearted bastards. Look at Drake. I loved him more than anything, and he just let me go. I hope he's enjoying the good life out in Los Angeles without me. I hope he finds some nasty groupie who gives him every STD known to man."

I was the biggest asshole in the world. I'd broken the heart of the only girl who I'd ever loved.

"Chloe, shut up!" Amber shouted.

"No, let her finish. I'm curious as to what else she has to say about me," I said, unable to stay quiet.

Amber sighed and moved, so Chloe could see me. When she turned around to look at me, her mouth dropped open in shock.

"In my defense, I tried to warn you," Amber said.

"I thought you said you got rid of him!" Chloe groaned.

"I said, I took care of it. There's a difference."

"Whatever. I'm done talking now. Both of you can go jump off a bridge."

"No, keep talking. I'd love to hear what else you wish upon my poor dick. That kind of hurts, you know. I'm quite fond of that certain body part." I smirked at her. I couldn't help but tease her.

"I want him out, Amber. Now," she growled.

"Just listen to him, please. If not for him, then do it for yourself. You deserve that much," Amber pleaded.

I watched as Chloe looked back and forth between Amber and me. I could practically hear the wheels spinning in Chloe's head. I just hoped that she would give me a chance to talk.

"You have five minutes. After that, I'm kicking you out," she finally said.

"Works for me. I'm late for my party, so I'll catch you two later." Amber winked at Chloe.

I waited until Amber walked out the front door before I turned to face Chloe. "Did you really want me to catch a bunch of sexually transmitted diseases?"

"You're wasting your five minutes. I'm waiting." Chloe crossed her arms over her chest and glared at me.

I couldn't help but smile at Chloe's stubbornness. It was one of my favorite things about her. I knew coming back here was a gamble, but I couldn't stop myself. I had to know if she still wanted me.

"I'm not going to lie. I was hoping you would welcome me back with open arms."

"Sorry to disappoint you. Why are you even here? Shouldn't you be out, snorting cocaine and banging groupies? I figured you were living the typical rock-star life by now," she snapped.

"Yeah, I guess I deserved that, didn't I?" I asked.

She raised an eyebrow but said nothing as she waited for me to continue.

"And I assumed it would be obvious why I was here. I've missed you."

"You've missed me? If you've missed me so much, why didn't you call me even once over the past six months?"

"Because I couldn't. After you left, things started to get worse, and I started using more. Then, Eric got the call about the label out in L.A. wanting us to come out and talk to them. My life went crazy from there."

"I was waiting for Jade or one of the guys to call me and tell me you were dead from an overdose, Drake. All this time, I've secretly worried about you, and you couldn't take two seconds out of your busy life to let me know you were okay. That's bullshit."

"At least that means you still care," I mumbled, feeling like the biggest ass ever. I never wanted to stay away from Chloe, but I had wanted the drugs more than anything.

"I did care, not anymore though. I've seen you, so you can go away now."

"Don't you want to hear anything that I came here to say?"

"Not really, Drake. You ripped my heart out once already. I don't need to go through that again."

"I never meant to hurt you. Honest. You're the most important thing in the world to me, but my judgment was clouded. I just miss you so much, and I know that I fucked-up."

"I don't know what you want me to say to that, Drake. I already made myself clear back on the bus. I don't want anything to do with you while you're on drugs. I can't stop you from destroying your life, but I can still save mine," she whispered as a tear slid down her cheek.

I wanted more than anything to wipe it away, but I knew she wouldn't let me. That wall she used to keep people away was up, and this time it was up for me. I hated to think that I had hurt her to the point where she might never let me in again.

"I'm clean, Chloe. I have been for a couple of months now."

"What? Why didn't you try to reach me then? Is it because you finally figured out you could do better than me?"

"You know better than that, Chloe. I love you. Basically, the band and our manager threatened to fire me from the band if I didn't get clean. I had already lost you, and they were the only things I had left that mattered. I checked myself into a two-month program, and I've been clean ever since."

"So, let me get this straight. You cared enough about the band to go into rehab, but I wasn't enough of a reason when I walked away from you?"

"No, it's not like that, Chloe. I knew I was in trouble, and it was just the final straw. I wanted to stay in the band, and I wanted to win you back."

"How do I even know you're telling me the truth about all of this? And if it is true, that means you've been out of rehab for a month without contacting me."

I knew she wouldn't believe me, so I had come prepared with help from Dr. Peters. I stood as I reached into the inside pocket of my jacket, and I pulled a piece of paper out. "If you want proof, then here it is. As for why I'm just now showing up, I wanted to make sure I could handle the outside world without falling back into my old habits. I didn't want to come back and tell you I was clean, only to disappoint you again."

She stood up and came a few steps closer to me. She stopped when she was close enough to grab the paper out of my hand. I waited while she read what I hoped was my saving grace. It was my certificate of completion from the rehab center in Los Angeles.

"You really did it then?" She stared down at the paper in her hands.

"Yeah, I did. You were all I thought about while I was in there. I screwed up so bad with you, Chloe, and I want to make it right. I want to make us right."

"It's not that simple, Drake. You really hurt me. You let me walk off that bus without even trying to stop me. I'm glad that you got help, but I don't think I can go through that again."

"I'm so sorry for what I did, Chloe. I promise you that I will never do anything like that again."

"How can you be sure, Drake? You're just starting out in an industry that is full of drugs and sex. Can you really walk side by side with temptation on a daily basis and not give in? Drugs will be easy to get, and women will be lining up for you. It'll be worse than when we were together. I can't handle that kind of life. I won't share you with them."

"Then, come with me. Stay by my side every night so that you know you can trust me."

"What?" Her eyes widened in shock.

"I said, come with me. That's why I came back, Chloe. I want you back, and I want you by my side through all of this."

"You can't just walk back into my life and expect me to drop everything for you, Drake. Even if I did want to give us another chance, I have responsibilities here, like school and my part of the rent for this place."

"So, stay here until you're finished with school for the year. Then, you can take online classes and come on tour with us. Thanks to me, we're still in the studio, recording tracks for our first album, and we will be there for a few months. We won't start touring until several months from now."

"This is insane, Drake!" she shouted.

"Please, Chloe. I love you. I want to spend every second of my life with you from now until the day I die. I can't live without you," I pleaded.

This had gone so much better in my head. While I knew she would be angry, I had hoped that I wouldn't have to resort to groveling to get her to take me back. If I had to though, I would. I would rather die than spend one more day without her.

"I don't want to get hurt again, Drake," she whispered. "I can't take it."

I grabbed her and pulled her into my arms. She struggled at first, but I held on tight, refusing to let her go.

"I will never hurt you again, Chloe. Never. Let me prove it to you."

I pressed my lips to hers and kissed her like I was dying, like it was the last kiss we would ever share because it might just be our last. When I let her go, she might slap me and then never speak to me again. If she did, I wanted to remember the feel of her lips against mine for the rest of my life.

Despite what she'd said, her body responded to me instantly. She wrapped her arms around me and kissed me back, showing me just how much she still wanted me. I groaned as her lips parted, and I slipped my tongue inside her mouth, flicking my tongue ring against her tongue in a way that I knew drove her crazy.

She moaned in response before quickly pulling away. "What are we doing?"

"I'm not sure what you were doing, but I was kissing the woman I love."

"I love you, too, Drake, and I do want to be with you. There's no way that I can deny that now, but if we do this again, we're going to take it slow and start over. I don't know how this is going to work with you being so far away though."

A smile broke out across my face. If I had known a kiss was all it would take to change her mind, I would have done that first.

"We'll figure it out. We always do." I kissed her softly. "But I can't agree to the taking-it-slow part."

"Why not?" she asked, confused.

I reached into my pocket and pulled out a small box. "After I checked out of rehab, the first thing I did was stop at the jewelry store, and I picked this up."

Her mouth dropped open as I lowered myself to one knee and opened the box to reveal a sparkling diamond ring.

"Oh my God," she whispered.

Before I met Chloe, if someone told me I would be down on one knee, asking the woman I loved to marry me, I would have kicked that person's ass. Before her, marriage had been nothing more than a trap that others fell into. I was too smart for that, or so I had thought.

"Chloe Marie Richards, I never thought I would ever be one of those dumbasses who loves a woman so much he wants to tie himself to her forever, but here I am, down on one knee, trying to think of something sweet and romantic to say. As you can tell, I'm failing miserably, so will you please put me out of my misery and say yes if I ask you to marry me?"

She laughed as I stared up at her.

"I don't know. You'll have to ask me to find out."

"I thought I just did."

"No, you asked me if I would say yes if you asked me to marry you. It's not the same."

I groaned. "You're not going to make this easy on me, are you?"

"After the last six months? I think not. You're lucky that I haven't thrown you out yet."

"Fine. Chloe, will you please marry me? I promise to love and cherish you forever and always, and I promise to give you lots of mind-blowing sex every day."

"Even when we're ninety and walking with canes?" she asked with a serious look on her face.

"Damn it, quit stalling! Will you marry me or not?"

"Well, since you asked me so nicely, I guess I have to now." She laughed.

"That was a yes, right?"

"That was a yes."

I let out a breath I hadn't realized I had been holding as I pulled the ring from the box and slipped it onto her finger. "Thank God."

"Aren't you going to kiss me or something now? You're not very good at this, you know."

"I was getting to that part, smart-ass." I stood back up and pulled her into my arms. "I can't wait until you're Mrs. Drake Allen. Hell, maybe even one day, we will have two-point-five children and live in a log cabin by a lake."

She grinned. "I never understood that whole point-five thing, but I wouldn't mind kids someday. I love you, Drake. I don't think I could be any happier than I am right now."

"Me, too, baby. Me, too." I attacked her mouth.

I was going to make up for every lost moment with her even if it took me all night or all year. I didn't care. I had her in my arms, and there was nothing in this world that would ever tear us apart.

I knew we had a lot to figure out, especially with me living in Los Angeles now, but I wasn't worried. Sometimes, life threw curveballs, but other times, it seemed like everything fell into place. I was determined to make sure Chloe had her happily ever after, starting right now.

PART TWO

Learning to Love Again

Chloe

Chapter 9

Three Months Later

I zipped the last bag and threw it on top of the pile of stuff sitting beside my bedroom door. This was it. I was really doing it. I was going to move across the country to be with Drake. I couldn't help but wonder if I'd lost my damn mind. I was giving up everything to take a chance on someone who had broken me. I loved him though, and I knew in my heart that I was doing the right thing. We still had so many issues to work through, but I was willing to try if it meant spending the rest of my life with him.

Three months had passed since he'd appeared on my porch after over six months of no contact. The next day, he'd gone back to Los Angeles to record more songs for the album. Since then, he had tried on more than one occasion to get back to me, but it hadn't worked out. With the album, photo shoots, promotions, and everything else they could throw at him, the label had kept him busy constantly, so he hadn't been able to leave. We'd talked several times a week, but it hadn't been the same.

Now, I was going to be with him daily. We'd done little to work through our issues. We hadn't wanted to do it over the phone, but we could finally start now. I wasn't sure if moving in with him while working on our relationship was going to be a good thing or not. I just hoped that it would be. I wanted things to go back to the way they had been between us. I was starting to heal from what he had done, but I wasn't quite there yet. I needed to be with him, so we could do it together.

A knock sounded on my bedroom door, and Logan popped his head in. "You got a sec?"

"Sure. Come on in."

He stepped inside and closed the door behind him. "I see you're packed and ready to go."

I nodded. "Yeah, I just finished. I don't think it has sunk in yet that I'm actually leaving. It's going to be so scary to start over thousands of miles away from home."

He sat down beside me and pulled me close. "I'm going to miss you, Chloe. It won't be the same around here without you."

"Don't lie. You'll finally be rid of me. You're probably planning a party to celebrate my departure!" I joked.

"Not even close. I'm going to pop some popcorn and cuddle up with a blanket on the couch to watch Johnny Depp or some stupid girlie shit like that."

I laughed. "You will not watch Johnny without me. It's in our friendship code."

"I wouldn't watch it with you, so there's no chance I'm watching it without you. I hate that stupid pirate movie."

"Don't hate on Johnny. He helped me through some really rough times."

Logan's smile slipped a bit, and he squeezed me gently. "If something happens, call me. I'll find a way to get there to help you, okay?"

"Nothing is going to happen, so don't worry about me. Drake and I have a lot of work to do, but I love him, and he loves me. It's just going to take some time to get back to where we were. I lost my trust in him, and he lost himself."

"I know you love him. I just don't want to see you hurt anymore. Just promise me that you'll call me if something happens."

"I promise, but please don't worry about me. I'm a big girl. I can take care of myself."

"I know you can, but that doesn't mean I won't worry."

I knew he would worry. It was just the way he was. Logan was one of those people who cared so much that it killed him to see when his friends were hurting.

"I know. Just try not to though. Go out and get a girlfriend or something. You need to get a social life."

He elbowed me. "I do have a social life. I have friends. I'm just not interested in dating anyone right now. I need to focus on school."

"You're such an overachiever. Promise me that you'll try to get out more."

He sighed. "I will. You're a hard act to follow though, Chloe. Whatever girl catches my attention will have to work hard to be as cool as you are."

"I am pretty awesome." I paused, staring at Logan. "We're still good, aren't we? I mean, you don't think about me like that anymore, right?"

"You're nothing more than my best friend. I realized long ago that Drake was the one for you, and I've finally accepted that, but it doesn't mean I'm ready to move on. I'll get there, but it might be a while."

I hugged him tightly. "You're a great guy, and the girl who manages to snag you will be very lucky. I just hope she's good enough."

Amber opened my door, and we both looked up. "Drake just pulled in. You ready?"

I released Logan and nodded as I stood. "Yeah, I guess I am."

They followed me to the front door. When I opened it, Drake was standing there with his hand held up, getting ready to knock. The smile that broke across his face was infectious, and I found myself smiling back. He looked good. No, he looked amazing. The last time I'd seen him, he had looked good, but now, he was downright beautiful. He looked so happy, and knowing I was one reason for his happiness made my heart swell.

"Hi," I said lamely.

"Hi, back. I've missed you." He stepped closer and planted a kiss on my forehead.

We'd talked about toning down the physical part of our relationship and I was glad to see he was trying to keep his promise to be good. If he'd tried to kiss me, I know I would have caved right there. I'd missed his lips and his touch, and not having him now was a cruel torture. I wanted to do this right though, and that meant slowly building our relationship back to where it was. We were starting over even though I had his ring on my finger. I guess we were healing in reverse.

"You ready?" he asked.

I nodded as I stepped back to let him in. "Yeah, I have everything packed and ready to go. You just have to carry it to your car."

I had expected him to complain about carrying out my things. After all, I was packing up everything I owned, but he only nodded and walked down the hallway to my room. Logan followed, and a few seconds later, both reemerged with a few of my bags. Amber and I grabbed a few more, and we loaded them into Drake's car. I was glad he'd borrowed the label's private plane, or I would have been forced to ship everything. I could only imagine the charges.

"That's the last of it." Drake slammed the trunk of his car closed.

"Thank God," Logan grumbled.

I laughed and pulled Logan into a hug. "Thanks for helping."

"You're welcome, Chloe. Just take care of yourself, okay?" he whispered into my ear.

"I will. I love you, Logan."

"Love you, too. Now, go before I decide I want you to stay. I doubt Drake would appreciate it if I kidnapped you."

"No, I wouldn't," Drake said from behind me.

I turned to see him standing just a few feet behind us. He didn't look mad though. He seemed strangely calm around Logan. After everything happened between the three of us, the two of them had never really been able to hang around each other, but it was good to see that Drake was trying to accept Logan. I loved Drake, and I needed him to accept my friendship with Logan. He was trying, and that made me happier than I could have ever imagined.

I turned to see Amber watching me with tears in her eyes. "Don't cry, Amber. We'll see each other again."

"It's not the same though. I feel like I'm losing my best friend," she cried.

"You know you can come out to Los Angeles this summer, and I'll come back to visit, too."

"It won't be the same!" she whined.

She ran over to me and wrapped her arms around me. I hugged her tightly, afraid to let go. I knew it would be different. I was used to having Amber and Logan around constantly. I was going to feel lost without them.

Amber pulled away. "Go. I don't want any long, drawn-out good-byes. It'll just make me miss you more."

I nodded as I waved at both of them. I got into Drake's car and turned in my seat as Drake started the car. As he pulled away, I watched Amber and Logan until they disappeared from sight when the car turned the corner. A single tear slid down my cheek as I realized that I was losing two of my best friends. Sure, we would always be friends, but it wouldn't be the same with us living so far apart from one another. I just hoped that Amber and Logan took care of each other.

"You okay?" Drake glanced over at me.

"Yeah, it's just hard to say good-bye. I'm going to miss them so much."

"I know, but you'll still get to see them from time to time. Plus, you won't be alone once we get home. Jade will be there, and I know how much you like her." He reached over and squeezed my hand.

That was true. While Jade and I weren't best friends, like I was with Logan and Amber, I still loved her to death. We had been texting more since Drake had come back into my life, and she was excited that I was finally going to join them in Los Angeles. I thought she was secretly tired of hanging around just guys. I couldn't blame her though. If I had to deal with only Drake, Eric, and Adam all day, every day, I'd pull out my hair.

The car ride through town was silent and awkward. We'd talked a lot on the phone, but now, it was different in person. We both knew that we needed to have *that* conversation—the one where we laid all of our cards on the table—but neither of us wanted to bring it up. At least, I knew I didn't. It was going to be painful to talk about everything that had happened in the months leading up to our breakup, and I wasn't quite ready to dredge up those memories.

I picked up my phone and started playing on it just to do something other than sit quietly. After checking my emails, I glanced up to see that we were already on I-79. When we passed a sign indicating we were going south instead of north to the airport in Pittsburgh, I looked at Drake.

"We're going the wrong way," I said.

"Are we?" He grinned.

"Um, yes. I thought you said we were going to Pittsburgh to fly back to Los Angeles. We need to go north, not south. You're heading toward Charleston."

"My bad." He stared straight ahead.

"Drake, where are we going?"

"I thought it might be nice to take a road trip." He glanced over at me. "That way, we can have more time alone together before I have to go back to work."

"We're driving to L.A.? That will take days!" I exclaimed.

"That's the point. I told the label I wouldn't be back for a few days. They know that I'm not to be bothered."

My mouth hung open. "Can you even do that? I mean, isn't the label your boss?"

"They are, but we've all been working our asses off for them. Brad has been great, and he completely understood that we needed some time off."

"Look at you, throwing your rock-star weight around," I joked.

"Yeah, I'm a big bad rock star now. Bow down to me."

I rolled my eyes. "I remember having this exact conversation when you took me to get my tattoo. I didn't bow then, and I won't do it now."

He laughed. "I thought you might have hated me back then. It was so fun to mess with you."

"I never hated you. I just didn't like you."

Okay, that was a lie. Even then, I'd known that I was falling for this beautiful man. I just wasn't willing to admit that.

"Do you remember the time when we went with Amber and Logan to that dance club? Logan got wasted, and we had to drag him to his dorm room," I said.

"I remember that night, but it wasn't because I got to feel up Logan. I distinctly remember feeling you up," he said, still staring straight ahead.

I could never forget that night. It was the first time when I'd gotten a real chance to feel Drake's body against my own. That was a memory that would always be burned into my brain.

"I remember," I whispered, still thinking about the feel of his hands on me.

"We'll have to do that again sometime." He smirked at me.

"I thought we were taking it slow," I countered.

"We are. We weren't together back then, and you had no problem grinding your ass against my dick."

He looked at me with lust-filled eyes that I hadn't seen in a long time. I squeezed my legs together, surprised at how turned-on I felt from just his words. I was the one who had made the let's-go-slow rule, yet here I was, aching for his touch. It had obviously been way too long since I'd had sex. When I added the time up in my head, I realized that it had been over nine months since we'd been together. It was no wonder I was acting like a horny teenage boy.

My stomach clenched as I wondered if it had been as long for Drake. I hadn't asked if he'd been with anyone when we were apart. I was afraid of the answer he would give me.

"What's wrong?" he asked, noticing how quiet I'd become.

"Nothing," I lied.

"I know you well enough to know when something's bothering you, so tell me. We're starting over, remember? No more secrets."

I bit my lip, wondering how on earth I was supposed to ask him if he'd been faithful to me. "I…it's just…well, were you with anyone while we were apart?"

He tensed. "I wondered when this conversation would come up. I wasn't with anyone, but…"

Oh no, there was a but. I was afraid to ask, but I had to. "But what?"

He sighed as he ran his hand through his hair. "Right before I went into rehab, the band and I went to this club. I had too much to drink, and I was already high. A girl approached me, and she looked so much like you that I thought it was you."

"What happened?" I whispered.

"I don't remember it all, but I do know that I ended up in a back alley with her." He glanced over at me. "Nothing happened, I swear. I kissed her, but that was it. I kept calling her Chloe, and she got pissed off and left my drunk ass there."

I shocked us both by giggling. I threw my hands over my mouth to stifle the sound.

His eyes widened in shock. "That wasn't the reaction I had expected."

"I'm sorry. It's just so funny. The poor girl thought she'd landed a rock star, and you couldn't even remember her name." I laughed even though there was nothing funny about picturing him with someone else in an alley.

He chuckled. "I'm glad you find it more amusing than she did. The stupid skank left me nearly unconscious in a back alley by myself. Luckily, the guys and Jade came looking for me, and they got me back to my room."

"Was it bad?" I asked.

"When we were apart?"

I nodded.

"Yeah, it was bad. I don't really want to talk about it while I'm driving. I want to focus solely on us when we have that conversation, okay?"

"Sorry," I mumbled.

"Don't ever be sorry for asking me something. I promise that I'll tell you whatever you want to know, but not while I'm going seventy miles per hour down the interstate." He took my hand and held it up to his lips to kiss. "I've missed you."

"I've missed you, too."

"Glad to hear it. You know, I have to ask, too. Have you been with anyone since me?"

I glanced over at him. He was gripping the steering wheel so hard that his knuckles were turning white.

"I haven't. I went on a few dates, but I wasn't interested in anyone but you. You've ruined me for life."

He smiled as he eased his grip on the steering wheel. "You have no idea how happy that makes me. Every minute of every day, I wondered about what you were doing. I thought I was going to go nuts from picturing you with other guys."

I raised an eyebrow. Was he serious right now? I wasn't the one who was constantly surrounded by people throwing themselves at me.

He must have noticed the look on my face. "Okay, maybe you do know what I'm talking about."

"Um, yeah, I do."

We spent the rest of the drive to our first stop in silence as if we were both afraid to say something wrong. It seemed like we were teetering on the tip of an iceberg. With one wrong move, we'd come crashing down into a cold and unforgiving ocean of pain. I didn't know about him, but I didn't want to crash and burn. I wanted us to learn to trust again.

It was late evening when we exited the interstate and pulled into a small hotel. It was no Hilton, but it wasn't a hole-in-the-wall motel either. The lobby was clean and brightly lit with an older man sitting at the reception desk.

"Can I help you?" he asked as we walked up to him.

Drake glanced at me. "Do you want one room or two?"

I'd never even thought about that question. We were supposed to be taking it slow, and while sleeping next to one another wasn't something major, it also wasn't slow.

"Why don't we get a room with two beds? I suggested, happy with the compromise I'd come up with.

"Works for me." Drake turned back to the man in front of us. "One room, two beds."

The man tapped on his keyboard for a few seconds before frowning. "I'm sorry, but we are out of double-bed rooms. I do have two rooms with one bed available if you'd like."

Well, crap. Drake glanced at me and gave me a questioning look. I didn't know what to do.

"It doesn't matter to me," I said.

There—I was off the hook. Drake could decide how we slept.

He shrugged and turned back to the clerk. "We'll take one of those rooms then."

I hid a smile. I'd secretly hoped that he would say that.

The clerk took Drake's credit card. After he charged the room to it, he handed it back with two key cards. "Here you go. You're on the first floor. Just go down that hallway there, and it's the third door on the right."

"Thank you," I said.

I turned and followed Drake down the hall and into the room. We'd each brought a small bag inside, and we set them on top of the dresser. The room was just like the lobby. It was clean but not flashy. I liked it. I was sure that Drake was used to spending his nights in fancy hotels, but I preferred something simpler, and he knew that. I appreciated that he was staying here for me.

"Why don't you shower first? I'll call Jade and let her know we safely made it this far." He pulled his phone from his jacket.

"Sure." I pulled a pair of pajamas from my bag and walked to the bathroom.

I took a quick shower and returned to the room to see Drake lying on the bed with his eyes closed. I tiptoed quietly around the room, thinking that he had fallen asleep. I nearly jumped out of my skin when he spoke.

"I'm still awake, you know. You don't have to go into super-secret-ninja-stealth mode just for me."

I laughed. "Maybe I like being a ninja."

He rolled his eyes. "I'll be sure to get you a ninja outfit when we get back to L.A."

"Gee, thanks."

He stood and grabbed a few things out of his bag before walking to the bathroom and shutting the door. I threw the covers down and crawled into bed. I listened to the pipes whine inside the walls as I stared at the ceiling. I was suddenly nervous about sleeping in the same bed as Drake.

You have to take it slow. You have to take it slow. You have to take it slow. I repeated this mantra over and over inside my head. Hopefully, I could convince myself before Drake came back to bed.

I had just convinced myself that I would be good when he opened the bathroom door and stepped back out into the room. He was wearing only his boxers. I couldn't help myself as my eyes traveled down his body. He had always been fit, but it was obvious that he had been working out in L.A. His body looked incredible, and I suddenly felt inadequate, especially in my pajamas. How the hell was I supposed to measure up to him?

I glanced up at his face and noticed him watching me with a grin.

"See something you like?" he teased.

"You did that," I gestured to his almost naked appearance, "on purpose."

He wasn't playing fair.

"I did. I just wanted to see if I still had the same effect on you."

"Well, you obviously have your answer. I can't look away."

He grinned as he stalked toward me. "I was hoping you'd say that."

My eyes widened as he crawled across the bed until he was hovering over me.

"Wh-what are you doing?" I asked nervously.

"I don't know if I can take this slow. I want to kiss you until we don't know where we are. I want to feel you pressed up against me, skin-to-skin, heart-to-heart." He leaned down and ran his lips across my nose. I didn't breathe until he leaned away.

"We can't. We have too much to sort through still," I whispered as I stared at his lips.

"One kiss isn't going to hurt anything." He leaned down again, stopping just before his lips touched mine. "Just one kiss."

When his lips met mine, I closed my eyes. Electricity shot through my body, and I wrapped my arms around him, pulling him down on top of me. He ran his tongue along my lips until I opened them to allow him access. He moaned just before he slipped it inside. I shuddered when I felt his tongue ring. This felt amazing. How had I survived without this for so long?

My hands ran along his back, my nails digging into his skin. When my hips lifted to grind against him, he moaned again. I wasn't in control of my body anymore. He was.

He pulled back, breathing hard. "Damn it. You make me lose control too easily!"

I kept my eyes closed. I knew I'd be a goner if I saw his eyes darkened with lust. There would be nothing in this world that could keep me away from him. When he rolled off of me, I took a chance and peeked over at him. He was staring up at the ceiling, and his chest was rising and falling hard. With only his boxers on, it was apparent that he hadn't calmed down. I lifted my hand to wrap it around his shaft, but I caught myself at the last second. This wasn't how it was supposed to go. We had to work through everything before we took the next step.

"You okay?" I asked stupidly.

"No, I'm pretty sure I'll be walking around hard for the next week after that." He glanced over at me.

"Sorry," I mumbled.

"Don't be. I started it. I couldn't help myself. It's been so long since we…well, you know."

I grinned. "Since what?"

He reached over and began tickling my ribs. "Since we slept in the same bed. There—how's that for an answer?"

"Very good. I'm impressed," I teased as I squirmed to get away.

"I'm sure you are. Can I ask you something?"

"I don't know. Can you?"

He gave me a pointed look. "I'm serious."

"Sure. Go for it."

"Can I hold you? I won't do anything else. I swear. I just want to hold you while we sleep."

I smiled, touched by his sweetness. "I can live with that."

I rolled onto my side, facing away from him. He pulled me tight against him and wrapped his arm around me.

"Good night, Chloe. I love you," he whispered into my ear.

I love you, too, I said in my mind, unable to let myself speak the words just yet.

Chapter
10

I awoke the next morning with Drake's arm still holding me tight against him. Unwilling to give up the moment, I closed my eyes and scooted back closer to him. I'd missed this so much. There was nothing in this world like waking up with him beside me.

He shifted in his sleep, trying to pull me tighter against him.

"Chloe..." he mumbled, still asleep.

My heart soared. He was dreaming of me.

"Chloe, don't leave me. Please. I'll do better."

The waves of happiness came crashing down around me. He was dreaming about me leaving him, not about having me back.

He whimpered like a small child and cried out again. "Chloe! I love you! Don't go. I'll make it better."

Unable to let him go on, I rolled over and peppered his face with kisses. "Drake...Drake, wake up."

He opened his eyes, and then a smile slowly spread across his face. "You're still here."

"Of course I am. Where else would I go?"

"I don't know. I thought you left me again."

My heart broke as I stared at him. Vulnerability was written across his face. He loved me, and he was terrified to lose me again.

"I love you," I whispered, deciding to show my vulnerability as well.

He smiled as he leaned forward and kissed me lightly. "It seems like it's been forever since you said that."

"It feels like that to me, too. I've missed saying it."

"Well, I've missed hearing it." He grinned.

I reached up and cupped his face. He was beautiful. Even though it wasn't the manliest term to use, there were no other words to describe him. He tried to be a badass when others were around, but when it was just the two of us, he always let his guard down. Drake was far from innocent, but in this moment, he looked more innocent and vulnerable than I had ever seen him. And the best part was that this man was mine. This beautiful, kind, and loving man was all mine.

During the last few months we were last together, he had been a different person. I had only caught a glimpse of what he was like while he was using, and I hoped that man was dead and buried. The man in bed with me now was my Drake. "Are you ready to have *the* talk?" I asked.

I was mentally trying to prepare myself for what was to come. This was going to hurt a lot, but it had to be done.

"My uncle already beat you to it. We had *the* talk when I turned thirteen and realized that girls didn't have cooties."

I rolled my eyes. "Smart-ass. You know what I mean."

He pulled me close and kissed the tip of my nose. "Yes, but can I at least pee first?"

"Knock yourself out."

I sat up and grabbed the menu off the bedside table. After glancing through it, I called and ordered room service. I was shocked that this place actually had it. When Drake came back into the room, I went into the bathroom to freshen up.

A few minutes later, a knock came on the door. I opened it to see a man standing there with two trays of food on a cart. He walked into our room and left the trays next to the bed. Drake pulled a bill from his wallet and tipped him. When he was gone, we grabbed our trays and settled back into bed.

"Where do you want to start?" Drake asked around a mouthful of food.

"I don't know. I guess when you started using again. I feel like everything we talked about then is null and void now that I know you were stoned most of the time."

Drake hung his head in shame. "I'm so sorry."

"Don't apologize. You walked away from it. You're better now, and I'm so proud of you for it." I looked into his sorrow-filled eyes.

"I ruined everything, Chloe, and it was all because I thought you had cheated on me."

"I don't blame you for assuming the worst. Hell, even I thought those pictures looked bad, and I knew the truth."

"I could have stopped using once I knew the truth though...but I didn't. I thought I still had control of it, but I just kept going. I know now that I'd already lost control, even then."

I knew how hard this was going to be, but I hadn't realized how hard it would be to see Drake feel so disgusted with himself. He was so ashamed of what he had done, and I couldn't stand to watch him suffer.

"Never look at it that way. I'm so proud of you for getting clean and getting your life back on track. Give yourself some credit."

He looked away. "I guess. That's enough with the pity party. Let's move on."

I nodded. "You talk, and I'll listen. Just remember that I won't judge you for anything you tell me."

"When I thought you had cheated on me, I found a drug dealer and went to his place. The whole time when no one could find me, I was with him, stoned out of my mind. Then, you showed up and explained everything, but I was still upset about Jordan, so I kept using. I thought I had it under control. I convinced myself that I was using just to help me deal with Jordan's constant presence. I was sure that everything would be fine after you took him home and it was just the two of us again, but that didn't happen. Instead, your mom killed herself, and I wasn't there for you. I was off getting stoned while Jordan and Logan took care of you."

He leaned back against the headboard and blew his hair out of his eyes. It killed me to listen to him relive everything that had torn us apart.

"You don't have to tell me everything right now. We can stop whenever you want."

He shook his head. "No, I want to get it all out. We both need this."

"Yeah, we do," I said.

"Anyway, when I finally managed to get back to you, there they were, both watching out for you. Then, when I found out that Jordan had kissed you and you hadn't told me, I got pissed off all over again. By the time we finally left, I was using more, and I didn't want to stop. If I did, I knew I would have to face everything that was happening around us. We'd already been through so much, and I just wanted us to be happy with nothing hanging over our heads.

"You know what happened next. I started acting like an asshole—yelling at you and kicking the shit out of that guy in the bar. Then, you found my stash and told me it was over. I thought that you just needed to calm down, and then you'd come back. When you didn't, I realized that I'd really lost you, and I started using more.

"The next few months were bad, really bad. I tried to forget about you by using more, but it didn't help. You were always on my mind, and I hated myself for what I'd done. The band was pressuring me to get help, but I refused. Finally, it all came to a head one night at the club. I was already high when I got there, and then I drank too much. The guys had to haul my sorry ass back to the hotel. I *think* that I used again that night. I don't really remember doing it, and then the next thing I knew, I woke up in the hospital. The doctor told me that I'd overdosed, and if it wasn't for Jade coming in to check on me, I would have died."

My heart stopped. So, he had overdosed after all. All of those nights I'd spent awake, worrying about whether or not he was okay, were justified. He'd almost died. I'd almost lost the only person I ever loved, my soul mate.

He reached out and wiped away the tears running down my face. "Don't cry, babe. I'm okay now. If it wasn't for that night, I might still be using now. It was the wake-up call I needed to get my shit together. When I was in the hospital, I finally agreed to go into rehab. I won't lie. Those first few days of being clean were hell. I thought I was going to die from withdrawal. I felt sick, and I was mean to everyone. I just wanted to give up. But I kept thinking about you and what I would say to you when I finally saw you again. You kept me going even though I wasn't sure I had anything to look forward to. When I first went into rehab, I was an asshole to my doctor, Dr. Peters, but he didn't give up on me. He put up with all of my bullshit, and he helped me deal with not just my addiction but also the reasons I used drugs to begin with. I owe that man a lot."

I reached up and cupped his face. "I'm glad you had someone to help you. I always regretted leaving you to deal with

154

everything on your own, but I couldn't handle it. I had to protect myself."

"You did the right thing. You didn't need to be around me after everything that happened with your mom. I know that now, and I understand why you left the way you did. I have to ask you some questions though. What happened after you left me? Where did you go? What did you do?"

I knew he wasn't going to be happy with me, but we'd both agreed to no more lies even if we wanted to protect each other from the truth.

"I went back to Danny's house. Logan and Amber were still there, so I stayed with all of them until Logan and Amber were ready to go home. I was a mess, and Jordan took care of me. After we were back in Morgantown, Logan, Amber, and I found a place to live, and I started back at school. I used my classes to distract myself. Otherwise, I would have run back to you. I tried to live life and forget about you, but I couldn't. I looked for you in every face that passed by me. I was like an addict, too, and you were my drug."

He smiled. "I'm okay with you being addicted to me."

"I'm sure you are. I just…I don't know where to go from here. How do we heal?"

"Together. We heal together. The rest will fall into place." He picked up my left hand and stared at the ring shining brightly on it. "I was so afraid that you would say no when I asked you to marry me. I was sure that you were done with me."

"I would never say no, but I think we need to learn about each other again before we run off and get married. We have to make sure that this will work. We've both changed so much in the last few months."

"I agree, but I won't deny how happy I am to see that ring on your finger. You're mine and mine alone."

I smiled. "I am, and we'll work through everything. We've come too far to give up now. I want you to promise me something though."

"Anything." He played with the ring on my finger.

"If you ever feel like you're about to fall, tell me. I never want you to think that you have to handle your addiction on your own. I know you're clean, but the temptations will always be there, especially in your profession."

"I won't fall. There's no way that I'll ever go back," he said with determination.

"But if you ever start to feel the pull, tell me. I will help you through it. I promise."

"All right, I promise. I really think that I'm okay now though."

"I'm glad, but don't ever think that you have to hide anything from me."

He looked at me and smiled. "When did you get so smart?"

I elbowed him. "I've always been smart."

He laughed as he grabbed our now empty trays and set them on the cart. "And so humble."

I eyed him suspiciously as he crawled back into bed and pulled me closer to him.

"What are you doing?"

"We have to leave soon, so I want to hold you while I can. You never know what could happen between now and tonight. I might say something stupid, and you'll run away from me."

"I'm not running from you anymore. I think we've both done enough of that to last a lifetime." I scooted up a bit, so I was eye-to-eye with him. I brushed my lips against his in a gentle kiss—one of comfort, not of lust. "We're going to be okay."

He kissed me back. "We are."

We stayed in bed for a few minutes longer before finally crawling out and getting dressed for the day. We had everything packed up and in the car a few minutes later. I sat in the car and waited while he went to the main office and checked us out. As soon as he got into the car, he started it and took off for the interstate.

I felt myself relax as the miles slipped away. While it hurt to know how much pain Drake had endured by himself, it was something that I needed to know. We had to put the hurt, the anger, and the pain all out there, so we could heal and learn to trust each other again. While I knew it would take time for us to get back to where we had been, I felt whole again with him by my side. During all of those months apart, I had felt like I was missing a piece of myself. It was funny how one person could walk into your life and change everything about you.

I pulled myself away from my thoughts. "Why are you so quiet over there?"

Drake usually made small talk as he drove, but he'd been suspiciously quiet since we hit the Missouri state line a few miles back.

"Do you remember me telling you that I moved to West Virginia with my uncle after my parents died?" he asked.

I nodded. It seemed like years ago when we'd sat and discussed his parents near Cheat Lake, but I still remembered every little detail that he'd given me.

"Well, I'm originally from Missouri. My old house is only about an hour from here."

Now, I understood. He was silently mourning his parents and the childhood that he'd lost so long ago.

"Do you want to go see it? Or them?"

He gripped the steering wheel tightly. "I don't know. I'm not even sure if I remember where the house is or exactly where they're buried."

"Well, we could try to find them. Have you been back since…since you moved to West Virginia?"

He shook his head. "No, I haven't."

"Then, we'll try," I stated, more as a command than a suggestion.

"We'll try."

We spent the next hour in silence as I listened to my phone give directions to his old address. We pulled onto a street filled with middle-class houses, and then Drake parked across the street from a pretty white house.

"There it is." He stared across the street.

The house was similar to several houses on the street. It was a white two-story home with blue shutters and a massive front porch that had several baskets of flowers hanging from it. A child's swing set and a kiddie pool were in the front yard. There was a younger woman sitting on the porch, watching a little boy swinging with all of his might on the swing set.

"That was me so long ago, but the swing set was over there." He pointed toward a flower garden. "And our pool was in the backyard."

"It's a beautiful home," I said, unable to think of anything else to say.

"It is. It doesn't seem like I've been gone for ten years. I wonder what my room looks like now. Maybe it's his." He gestured to the little boy on the swing.

"Do you want to get out? I'm sure they wouldn't mind if we went over to talk to them and to see the house up close."

"No, it's their sanctuary now, not mine." He started the car and pulled away.

"Do you still want to visit your parents?" I asked.

"I don't know. I'm not sure if I can handle it."

"I'll respect whatever you decide, but I think you should. You need closure and I'll be right beside you if you need me."

He reached across the console and took my hand. "I know you will. I'll try, but if I want to leave, we leave. Deal?"

"Deal." I held his hand tightly.

The cemetery where they were buried was only a few miles from their house. Drake took a couple of wrong turns, but we eventually found it. It was small but well taken care of. We were both silent as Drake drove through the area until we stopped near the back.

"They're over there." He shut off the car.

"Do you want me to wait in the car or come with you?" I asked.

"I want you with me."

We both stepped out of his car and started walking toward the back row of stones. Drake held my hand tightly as if he were afraid that I'd leave him alone. I wouldn't leave him though. I knew he needed this to help him accept that they were really gone. He stopped when we reached a large stone with the name *Allen* written across the top of it. Underneath were his parents' names, *Diane and Landon.*

"There's nothing on their graves. We should've brought flowers or something," he said.

"I don't think they care about that. I'm sure they're just happy that you came back."

"I shouldn't have stayed away for so long. I just couldn't face coming here. I was just a kid when it happened, and then life started happening, and I pushed it away. Coming here makes it real. I can't pretend that it was just a bad dream. I'm staring at their fucking graves. Graves—that's all that's left of them in this world. How is that fucking fair? What did I do to deserve losing them?" With each spoken sentence, his voice grew until he was shouting.

I felt helpless as I watched him drop to his knees and fall apart beside me. He was in so much pain, and I couldn't do anything to help ease it. He'd pushed their deaths away for so long, and now, all of the pain and guilt was too much. It was crippling him.

I dropped down beside him and lifted his head with my hand. "Look at me. You did *nothing* to deserve losing them. *Nothing!* You were a child, Drake. This world can be a terrible place, and every day, people go through things that they shouldn't have to. You just need to remember that there are people here who care about you, and they want to help you heal."

"I'm so lost, Chloe. I think I always have been."

"I'll help you find your way. You are such an incredible person, and that shines through even when you try to hide it. None of us are perfect, and we never will be."

"I don't want to screw up and lose you again. I can't handle it."

"Don't be afraid of that. I'm not going anywhere."

Tears were sliding down his cheeks as he turned to look at his parents' graves. "Do you think they'd be proud of me? I've screwed up so much in my life."

"We all screw up. I think they would be proud of the man their son has become."

He pulled me against him and hugged me tightly. "Thank you for making me do this."

"You have to accept your past before you can move toward your future. Accepting their deaths is just one part of your past."

"I just miss them so much."

"I know you do. My mom was a terrible person, and I still miss her."

He smiled. "Only you could miss Andrea."

I sighed. "I know. I just can't help it. She was my mom even though she never wanted to be."

"Your problem is that you care too much." He kissed my forehead. "But it's a good problem to have."

"Thanks." I rested my head on his shoulder. "I'm going to go back to the car. You need time here by yourself. I'll be right there if you need me."

"Okay." He released me and turned back to the graves in front of us.

I stood and walked back to the car.

Chapter 11

I watched from the passenger seat as Drake sat down on the ground in front of his parents' grave. I could see his lips moving as he spoke to them, and I prayed that he took the time to say everything he needed to say. He needed this. He was so broken inside, but he always hid it so well. It was time that he let it all go before it destroyed him. After all, it nearly had. He'd almost lost everything because he refused to deal with the hard things in life.

I must have dozed off because I woke up when I heard Drake getting in and starting the car. I rubbed my eyes and stretched as he drove around the circle to get out of the cemetery. I felt like the worst girlfriend ever for sleeping when he needed me.

"Are you okay?" I asked.

"I will be."

"Do you want to talk about it?"

"Nah, I'm talked out at this point. I told them everything I had to say."

I grabbed his hand and held it tightly. "I'm glad."

"I think I needed that, so I could let go. I've been holding on to them for too long, and it was destroying me. Dr. Peters and you have helped me realize that. I said my good-byes, and now I need to move on."

"You never have to forget them, Drake. We can always come back whenever you want."

"I know."

My stomach started growling around the time we hit the Oklahoma border. Drake stopped at a small diner, and we spent over an hour there, just relaxing and enjoying our food. I'd noticed that he was taking his time with everything on this trip. It was like he was trying to prolong our time alone together for as long as possible.

When I asked him about it, he shrugged.

"We aren't part of the rest of the world until we get back to L.A. I don't want anything to interfere with us, and I know it will once we get back. I want to enjoy the time alone with you."

I smiled. There was my Drake. "I love you."

He gave me a strange look. "I love you, too. Why are you telling me now?"

"Because that was one of the sweetest things I've ever heard."

By the time we hit Tulsa, it was starting to get dark. I could tell that Drake was getting worn out from driving all day, and I asked him to stop for the night. He found a hotel that was much like the last one we'd stayed at.

We checked in and headed to our room. I grabbed my pajamas and went to take a shower. After being stuck in a car all day, it felt nice to stretch my muscles as I showered. The warm water was relaxing as it washed the day from my skin.

I finished my shower, dressed, and went back into the room. I settled down onto the bed as Drake took a shower. This time, he hadn't bothered with asking me if a single bed was okay. I didn't mind at all. I'd missed snuggling with him when we were apart. I kept telling myself that we had to take things slow, but I felt my resolve waver when he stepped out of the bathroom in only his boxers again. The fact that he'd opened up to me today, letting me see his vulnerable side, didn't help either. It made my plan ten times harder.

The Drake that had pushed me away was long gone, and my Drake was back. He was the one who had stolen my heart so long ago, and I couldn't deny him anything. I knew I'd had a good reason for needing to go slow, but as he lay down beside me, I couldn't seem to think of it.

"I'm beat." He yawned.

"Why don't you let me drive tomorrow?"

"I might take you up on that, but you have to sign a waiver before I let my baby go."

165

I rolled my eyes. "It's just a car."

"It's my baby. Period."

"Men," I grumbled as I rolled over and snuggled up to him.

"I'm only kidding. You know I trust you with my car. It's Adam who I would never let behind the wheel." He shuddered visibly.

He wrapped his arm around me and kissed the top of my head. This was heaven. I relaxed further into him as I drifted off to sleep.

I woke up the next morning to Drake rubbing small circles across my lower back. I kept my eyes shut, knowing that he would stop if he knew I was awake. He pushed my shirt up as he started rubbing higher and higher. He moved his hand back down, so it was resting on my hip as he continued to make those circles across my skin. I squeezed my eyes shut while I tried to keep my breathing under control. God, I'd missed his touch so much.

When he scooted closer, I could tell just how turned-on he was. I felt the length of him pressed against my bottom. He was hard and ready. I couldn't stop the tiny moan that escaped my lips.

His hand froze. "Are you awake?" he whispered.

"Nope," I mumbled back.

He leaned in and kissed the back of my neck. "Faker. How long have you been awake?"

"Long enough to know you were feeling me up."

"I was not feeling you up. I was rubbing your back."

"But you wanted to feel me up." I rolled over to look at him.

"True, but I was trying to follow your rules."

I studied him closely. "It's driving you nuts, isn't it? Not being together, I mean."

"It is, but I understand why you're doing this. You don't want us to move too fast before we get back to the way we were."

I sighed. "It's that, but a part of me is afraid that I'll get too close to you too fast. I just don't want to get hurt again. We both promised to go slow when you asked me to marry you. Healing in reverse, remember?"

He cupped my face as he kissed me gently. "I'll never hurt you again."

"I love you, Drake, so much."

"I love you, too. No matter what happens, you'll always have me."

I pulled him closer and kissed him deeply. I couldn't help myself. No matter how many times I'd told myself to take things slow, it just wasn't happening. We'd been apart for so long, and enough was enough. Besides, I could never deny Drake. Since day one, I couldn't stay away from him. Even in the beginning, nothing had ever been slow with Drake and me. From the first time we met until everything came crashing down around us, our entire relationship had moved at warp speed. That was just how we were, and nothing would ever change that, no matter what we did.

I parted my lips, and his tongue slipped inside. I moaned as I felt his tongue ring against my tongue. That damn thing was so fucking erotic. His hand went back to rubbing my hip as I ran my nails down his back. He pulled away and started kissing my neck before he moved toward my ear.

"What are we doing?" he whispered.

"Kissing," I replied.

"We're moving in another direction here, and I need to know if it's okay. I'll stop if it's not."

"I don't want to stop," I said and I meant it.

"Thank God," he said. He started kissing my lips again. "If you told me to stop, I was going to go crazy. I want you so fucking bad."

There were no words for a while after that. After he pulled off my shirt and tossed it aside, his hands roamed across my body. I sucked in a deep breath when he flicked his tongue across my nipple. He took his time exploring my body with his mouth before he found my breast again. I dug my nails into his back as he started sucking and biting. He released my nipple and started kissing down my stomach.

"Hands above your head," he said.

"I can't," I mumbled. I raised my arms and started running my fingers through his hair.

He looked up at me. "I told you a long time ago that I would tie you up if you didn't listen to me."

"You wouldn't dare."

He laughed. "I would, but not yet. One of these days though, I will. That's a promise."

A shiver ran through my body at the thought. I wanted him to, badly, but I wasn't ready for that just yet.

I nodded. I felt vulnerable and exposed when we were together like this, but then again, I always did when I was with Drake. He had every part of me—my heart, my soul, and my body. So yes, I was always vulnerable when it came to him. I tried to calm my racing heart as he started kissing me again.

He ran his tongue between my breasts and then slowly down my stomach to where my sleep shorts were sitting low on my hips. He used his teeth to slowly pull them down, and I lifted my hips to help him. When they were gone, he pulled off my underwear next. I felt the impulse to cover myself, but I didn't. I loved him and I wouldn't let my shyness get in the way of our healing. Or the awesome sex that was about to happen.

When he sat up and stared down at my naked body, I felt my body respond instantly to the lust in his eyes. My core was aching, and my nipples tightened almost painfully. It had been far too long since we'd been together.

"You're so goddamn beautiful. You're mine, Chloe, and if anyone ever touches you, I'll kill them. I won't lose you again."

Before I could respond, he pushed apart my legs and lowered himself between them. When his tongue swiped against my clit, my entire body came up off the bed as I shouted his name. He ran his tongue back and forth before thrusting it into me. I couldn't stop myself as my hips came up off the bed to meet him each time. As he tongue-fucked me, he started rubbing his thumb against my clit. The world exploded before my eyes as I came. I lowered my hands and grabbed his hair, holding him in place.

Before I could recover, he forced my hands to let go of his hair as he stood up. I couldn't look away as he pulled off his boxers. I felt my cheeks turn red as I stared at him, all of him. He smirked at me as he climbed back into bed with me. He hovered over me long enough to kiss me before he slipped himself inside me.

"Oh my God!" I managed to gasp out as he entered.

It had been a long time, and it hurt as he thrust into me. Once he was fully inside me, he stopped, giving me time to get used to him again.

He moaned. "Jesus, you're so fucking tight."

"I'm sorry. I know it has to be hurting you, too. I haven't been with anyone since you," I whispered.

"It's a good kind of pain. I love that you've not been with anyone else. This," he said, pulling out and thrusting back in deeply, "is mine and mine alone."

"I'm yours. There was never any question of that."

He started thrusting again, slowly at first to let me get used to his size. He took his time working me to the brink and then stopping just before I came. This was the most beautiful form of torture that I could think of.

"Please stop teasing. I can't take it anymore," I pleaded.

"All you have to do is tell me what you want." He started kissing my neck.

"You know what I want. You always have."

"I want to hear you say it. I *need* to hear you say it."

He lowered his head down to suck on my nipple. He was still inside me, and I squeezed my muscles around his shaft.

A gasp escaped him. "Fuck!" he growled.

"Drake, please."

"Tell." Thrust. "Me." Thrust. "What." Thrust. "You." Thrust. "Want."

His thrusts were shallow, teasing. I tried to wiggle my body closer to his, but it was no use. I was at his mercy.

"I want you to fuck me!" I finally yelled.

"That's all I needed to hear."

With that, the teasing was gone. Drake started thrusting hard and fast into me, over and over again. I wrapped my legs around his waist to allow him to go deeper. My fingernails dug into his shoulders. I knew that I was going to leave marks, but I didn't care. I could feel myself ready to explode, but I held back. I didn't want this to end.

"I love feeling you so tight and hot around me. I could die right now and be okay with it. I can't think of a better way to go," he growled as he continued to pound into me.

"I can't hold on much longer," I gasped out.

"Let go!"

I shook my head. I didn't want this to end.

He smiled deviously. "Fine, make me work for it."

I didn't think he could go any harder, but he did. I screamed out as the force of his thrusts pushed me farther up the bed. Jesus, I couldn't hold on. I felt his piercing hit that one special spot over and over. I came, screaming, as I clawed at his back. He continued to pound into me as I came until he couldn't hold back any longer. With one final thrust, he came.

We were both gasping for breaths, and our bodies were slick with sweat. My body felt like jelly as I lay there, trying to remember how to breathe properly. I'd been with Drake so many times, but those times were nothing compared to this.

"Fuck!" Drake shouted, lifting his head to look at me. "You're still on birth control, aren't you? I didn't even think to ask."

"Now is a good time to think of it," I teased.

"Chloe…"

"Relax. There are no babies in your future."

"Good. I'm sorry that I didn't think to ask you. I just needed you so badly. That was unfuckingbelievable."

"I agree." I said against his lips as he kissed me softly.

"Not that I wouldn't want kids someday, but right now isn't the best time." He added, looking guilty.

"I knew what you meant." I smiled up at him.

He slowly pulled out and settled down beside me. I curled up against him, loving the feel of his skin on mine. I could feel his heart racing in his chest as I laid my head down on him. Lying next to him was pure bliss. Sex hadn't made things worse for us. Instead, it made things better. Being physically connected to him was as important as being mentally connected. We needed both halves to make us whole.

"I need a shower. I'm all sweaty," I said a few minutes later.

"Me, too, but let's hurry because we have a long way to go until our next stop. We'll probably drive through most of today and part of the night."

After about an hour or so of being on the road, we stopped at a drive-through and grabbed breakfast. I was shocked when Drake actually let me drive his *baby* most of the day. I nearly laughed when I saw him wince as he handed the keys over to me.

"I promise I won't scratch her. Chill." I teased as I sat in the driver's seat.

He grumbled as he sat down beside me. "If you do, I'll leave you beside the road."

There was a happiness surrounding us both that hadn't been there the day before. It was like we both finally realized that we would be okay. Or maybe we were both still high off of our awesome morning together. Either way, I wasn't complaining.

By the time late afternoon rolled around, my eyes were starting to grow heavy. I wasn't used to driving this long and I was desperate for a break. Drake seemed to notice and after we grabbed something else to eat, he happily took over the driving as I took my rightful place in the passenger seat and napped on and off as the miles passed.

I woke up in complete darkness. The clock on the dash said it was after midnight.

"Where are we?" I asked.

"Somewhere in eastern Arizona. I had to pull off for gas, but I didn't realize how far off the exit the damn station was. I've been driving down this little two-lane road for the last ten minutes, and I still haven't found it. I haven't even passed another car."

"Oh. Don't you think we should rest for the night? We've been driving forever, and we're both tired. Maybe there is a hotel around here."

"We will once we get a little farther. I was hoping to make better time, but we left late this morning."

I grinned. "That was my fault."

"Don't worry. I'm not complaining." When lights appeared in the distance, Drake relaxed. "Finally. I was starting to wonder if I had gone the wrong way."

The gas station was small but brightly lit. I waited in the car as Drake pumped gas and went inside to grab us both coffees. We were going to need it if we wanted to make it any farther tonight. I was thinking about our morning together when Drake came back to the car.

He noticed the smile on my face and gave me a questioning look. "Why are smiling?"

"Just thinking about this morning."

He grinned as he pulled back onto the dark road. "That's a good reason to smile. We should find a hotel for a repeat performance."

A thought struck me, and my smile widened. "You know, you always said you wanted to have sex in your car."

His head snapped over to look at me. "Don't tease me."

"Who said I was teasing?" I asked.

"You wouldn't do it," he replied, sounding sure of himself.

"Pull over and I'll prove it to you."

"Nope. I'll pull over, and you'll just laugh at me. I'm not falling for it."

"Suit yourself." I unbuckled my seat belt.

"What are you doing?" he asked.

I ignored him as I climbed over the center console and situated myself in his lap, facing him. He gripped the steering wheel tightly as I started kissing his neck. I moved up to his ear and bit down gently on his lobe.

"Fuck!" he growled.

I felt the car pull off the road and come to a stop.

"You could at least wait until I stop the car."

"You said you weren't going to pull over." My tongue probed inside his ear.

"I thought you were kidding."

I smiled as I moved back down to his neck. I had no idea what had come over me, but I wanted this. I wanted Drake to have everything from me that he'd ever dreamed about. I sat up and slowly unbuttoned his shirt. As soon as the last button was free, I started kissing down his chest. I ran my tongue over his nipples, tugging on his piercings with my teeth. When a growl escaped his mouth, I smiled.

I could feel his hardness straining against me. I reached down between us, undid his pants, and wrapped my hand around his shaft. He hissed as I started stroking him.

"God, that feels good," he moaned.

I freed him from his boxers as I continued stroking. I was wearing a skirt, so I pushed my underwear to the side as I started rubbing his dick against my clit. We both moaned at the sensations running through our bodies. I leaned back, so I had more room to move around. I yelled as I hit the car horn, and we both froze.

Drake started laughing. "You're an idiot."

"Sorry. I don't have much experience with car sex. I forgot about the car horn," I grumbled.

I covered his mouth with mine and slipped my tongue inside, effectively ending his laughter. My other hand reached up to flick his nipple ring while I continued stroking him. As I bit down on his lower lip, I could tell his breaths were growing ragged.

"You're just teasing me," he whispered.

"I'd never tease." I sat up maneuvered my body so that I could guide him inside me.

He grabbed the bottom of my shirt, lifted it over my head, and threw it on the passenger seat. His hands undid the clasp on my bra, and then he slipped the straps off my shoulders. He tossed the bra into the seat with my shirt, and then his mouth attacked my breasts. His tongue flicked across my nipple before he bit down gently. When he started sucking on it, I arched my back to give him better access. Then, I lifted myself up and slammed my body back down on his shaft. I started slowly, giving us both time to build up to our release.

"You can do better than that." He grabbed my hips and slammed me down on him.

I couldn't contain my moans as he lifted me and slammed me back down again. He was in control even though I hadn't planned it that way. My body rose and fell in rhythm with his. Every time he thrust up, his piercing hit that one special spot. I felt my orgasm building as he filled me over and over again. God, this felt incredible.

When his thrusts started to become erratic, I knew he was close. I ground my hips down hard, taking him by surprise. He shouted out my name as he lost control and came. I followed right behind. I laid my head on his shoulder as my body convulsed around him. I refused to move away until our bodies relaxed and our breathing returned to normal. I loved being this close to him.

"Thank you." He kissed my cheek.

"For what?" I teased.

"For trying something out of your comfort zone for me."

"I'd try just about anything for you."

When I sat up, the movement caused his dick to twitch inside me. I needed to return to my seat before he decided he wanted to go again. He helped me as I slid off his lap and went back into my seat. I grabbed my bra and shirt and started putting them back on as he buttoned his shirt and pants back up.

He watched me pull my shirt over my head. "You could always leave those off. I wouldn't mind."

"I'm sure you wouldn't."

Chapter 12

Drake finally gave in and stopped at a small hotel for the night, even though he wanted to keep going. We were exhausted from the long drive, and we crashed the minute we walked through the door.

When I opened my eyes, it was almost two in the afternoon. I groaned as I rolled over to look at Drake. I panicked for a moment when I saw that his side of the bed was empty, but I relaxed when I heard the shower. I stared up at the ceiling as I waited for him to finish, so I could shower before we left.

These last few days with Drake had been incredible, and I wasn't ready to join the rest of the world again. Once we made it to L.A., I knew Drake would be busy, and we wouldn't be able to spend as much time together as I would like. The band would start touring soon, but at least, I would be able to travel with him.

We'd had several conversations about what would happen once the band went on tour. Two of my major concerns were my college education and the groupies who were sure to be around constantly. The first had caused a bit of tension between us because Drake wanted me to quit school, but I wouldn't do it. He constantly told me that he would take care of us financially, but I didn't want to take a chance. Sure, I had the money my aunt had left me, but I didn't want to touch it if I didn't have to. If something were to happen between the two of us, then I'd be alone with no hope of finding a decent job. It wasn't that I didn't have faith in us. I just wanted to stand on my own two feet. I'd turned to Drake for a lot of things in life, especially after everything with my mom, and I didn't want to become completely dependent on him. After several small arguments, we'd both agreed to compromise. I wouldn't attend a traditional college. Instead, I would do my classes online. That way, I would still be in school, but I could travel with him on the tour bus.

There was no true resolution for my second concern. We both knew that groupies would hang around, and neither of us could do anything about it. I just had to accept the fact that they would be a part of his life, and I would have to trust that he wouldn't betray me. After everything that we'd endured, I trusted him. I just needed the voices in my head to shut up and go along with my decision.

Drake walked back into the room. "What are you concentrating on over there? You look like you're in deep thought."

"Nothing important," I answered.

"Chloe, you can tell me anything. What's making you frown like that?"

I sighed. "The usual. I was just thinking about how I'll deal with all the girls who will show up when you start touring."

He ran his hands through his wet hair as he sat down next to me. "Babe, we've talked about this. No one will ever compare to you. I just got you back. I'd never give up what we have for one of those girls."

"I know, but it still sucks."

"It does, but it's a part of this life. You've handled it well so far."

"Yeah, but it's going to be ten times worse now that you're a big-time band. Girls will be lining up to meet you, and most of them won't be wearing very many clothes."

"I've seen you naked. Nothing compares to that." He grinned down at me.

"You're such a charmer."

"I know. It's one of the many things you love about me." He leaned down and kissed me. "Now, get your stinky ass to the shower. We need to go."

"I do not stink!" I smacked him.

"Sure you don't. Go shower."

I rolled my eyes. "Fine." I stood and grabbed a set of clothes to change into after my shower.

We were back on the road. Time seemed to speed up since I wanted it to slow down. Before I knew it, we were passing a sign welcoming us to California. I couldn't help but feel a small twinge of excitement as we passed into my new home state. I'd traveled with my mother several years earlier, but this was the farthest I'd ever been from West Virginia. I knew I was in for a culture shock, and I was trying to prepare myself for it.

The closer we got to L.A., the quieter I became. My nerves were starting to get the better of me, and I couldn't seem to get my leg to stop jumping.

"Hey, are you okay?" Drake asked.

"I'm fine. I'm just nervous."

"Don't be. The band is excited that you're joining us, especially Jade."

"I can't wait to see them. I've missed them."

"You mean a lot to them. Adam even seems to like you."

I laughed. "Gee, what a compliment."

"With him, it is. He doesn't like many girls."

"What about Amber? Does he like her?"

Drake was silent for a minute before answering. "I don't know what's going on with those two. Amber is your friend, so I try to stay out of it."

"I just don't want him to hurt her. She says nothing is going on between them, but she gets this stupid dreamy look on her face when I mention him. I'm pretty sure that they're still talking."

"Adam doesn't talk to girls. If he's talking with her months after they've been around each other, something is going on with them. I just don't know how he'll handle it. Adam's past isn't that great."

I didn't know much about any of the band members' pasts. I never thought it was my place to ask, but his comment intrigued me.

"Why? What happened?"

"It's not my place to say. All of us have pasts where we've dealt with bullshit. The guys and Jade are good people despite the things they've had to deal with."

"I had no idea. They've never mentioned anything before."

"There are things that people try to forget. It's not that they don't want you to know, it's just the simple fact that they don't like to think about it."

"After growing up with my mother, I can understand that."

He glanced over at me. "Is there anything you haven't told me?"

I sighed. "There are things that I haven't told anyone. You know most of it though."

He reached over and took my hand. "If and when you're ready, you know I'm here. We're a team, and I'll help you through anything."

"I know. I just want to put it behind me. We're out here, thousands of miles away from home, and it's time to start fresh."

"You're right on everything except for the home part. We're not thousands of miles from home. We are home. This is our home now."

"True, but West Virginia will always be my home. Everything important to me happened there. We met there."

"And now we'll spend the rest of our lives together, doing whatever the fuck we want, wherever we want."

I laughed. Leave it to Drake to ruin a sentimental moment with his sarcasm and use of foul language. He had accomplished one thing at least. I wasn't nearly as nervous as before.

That changed when we hit L.A. city limits and my stomach did a nervous little flip. I watched in awe as Drake weaved through traffic like he'd been doing it all his life. We finally managed to break free from the traffic jams, and we were now on a highway where the traffic was actually moving.

As soon as I'd agreed to move out here with him, Drake had broken the lease on the apartment Jade had gotten him while he was in rehab. He'd bought a house, but I knew nothing about where it was at or what it looked like. I had secretly hoped that it wouldn't be right in the middle of Los Angeles, and when we arrived, I was glad to see that it wasn't. It was in one of the less populated areas of town. As we drove slowly down the street, I saw kids playing outside. It seemed like the type of neighborhood that had families instead of crazy rock stars. It was perfect.

Drake pulled into the driveway of a large, simple home. I should have expected something like that from him. He wasn't the type to go for flashy. It was a white two-story house with a black roof. It had a small front porch with a high privacy fence extending all the way around the house. The only hint that someone important lived here was the keypad on the gate and the fence.

"Welcome home," Drake said.

We grabbed a few of my bags and walked to the front door. I smiled as he unlocked it and held it open for me. As soon as I was through the door, I noticed a banner hanging from the staircase to the wall beside it. *Welcome home, Chloe!* was written across it. Out of nowhere, Adam, Eric, and Jade appeared. They were all grinning from ear to ear as they walked toward us.

"Chloe! I missed you!" Jade squealed as she ran forward and hugged me.

"I missed you, too." I hugged her back.

I really had missed her and the guys. I hadn't realized what a big part of my life they were until they were gone.

"It's good to have you back," Eric whispered as gave me a quick one-armed hug.

"It's good to be back," I whispered back.

Adam surprised me by grabbing me and literally throwing me into the air. "It's about time you got your ass back here. Now, maybe Drake won't be such a moping loser."

Drake rolled his eyes as he watched our exchange. "You're an ass."

"I try."

"What are you guys doing here?" I asked.

"Drake texted Eric when you guys got to L.A. We put the banner up yesterday, so we came over to chill until you got here," Adam said.

"We didn't want to miss your homecoming," Jade added.

"And Drake said something about all of us going out for dinner. I swear he mentioned he was going to pay, too." Eric grinned at Drake.

"You guys are only here because you want free food," Drake grumbled.

"I'm offended," Adam said as he pretended to be shocked.

"Sure you are. Why don't you and Eric make yourselves useful and carry the rest of Chloe's bags in while I show her our room?"

"We're guests. We don't have to do anything." Adam grinned.

Eric smacked him across the head. "Come on, asshole. Let's go get her stuff."

"I'll hang out down here until you guys are ready to go. There's a box on your bed. Make sure you put it on for tonight," Jade said.

She walked into the living room and sat down on a black leather couch. I raised an eyebrow. I loved Jade, but I wasn't sure how I'd feel about something she had bought me. I was kind of picky when it came to clothes.

"Okay," I said.

I followed Drake up the stairs to the second floor. We walked down a hallway until we reached the door at the very end. He pushed open the door and went in, setting down one of my bags that he'd carried up. Our room in his house back in West Virginia had been almost completely empty, but this one was filled. The walls were covered in photos of Drake and me and of the band. There was also a plaque with their first album that would be releasing soon. Stepping into his room was like I had walked into one massive photo album.

"Wow." My mouth dropped open in shock.

"I guess I got kind of carried away with the pictures."

"No, I love it. Before, it was like you lived in your head. You were afraid to hold on to anything sentimental, but this," I said, gesturing around the room, "is incredible. It's like you're opening up and showing the world who you are and what you care about."

He was silent as I walked around the room, looking at each picture. One in particular caught my attention. I reached up and took it off the wall to get a better look. It was a family photo. A man with coal black hair was standing behind a woman with flowing blonde hair. She was holding a dark-haired toddler in her lap.

"Is this your family?" I asked.

I knew it was, but I wanted confirmation. I could see so much of Drake in both of his parents. While it was obvious that he

187

looked mostly like his father, his mother's eyes were identical to his.

"It is. This was taken when I was two."

"You guys look so happy. And you look so much like your dad."

"We were. I wish I could go back to when that picture was taken and then relive every moment after. I'd cherish them so much more."

"Hold on to the memories you do have. They're never truly gone if you remember them."

He took the picture from me and placed it on a desk next to me. "Thanks, babe. You always know what to say."

I shook my head. "I really don't. I fly by the seat of my pants most days, and I just say whatever comes to mind."

He laughed. "Well, you do a pretty damn good job. Why don't you get changed and meet us downstairs?"

"Okay. I'm afraid to open Jade's box."

"She knows what you like."

"I hope so. I spent too many years being dressed by Amber to start that disaster all over again."

He chuckled as he left and closed the door behind him. I eyed the box on the bed warily as I approached it. I lifted the lid carefully, praying that Jade hadn't screwed me over. I felt a sense of dread when I saw all the fluffy paper hiding my present. From the packing, it was obvious that the gift was expensive. I held my breath as I moved aside the paper. I relaxed when I saw whatever was in the box was black. I hated bright colors, and Jade knew that.

I pulled it slowly from the box. My mouth dropped open in shock when I saw a gorgeous black cocktail dress. It had an emo-gothic feel to it, and I loved it. I pulled off my clothes and slid into it. It fit perfectly. I walked to a wall mirror and stared at my reflection. Despite my crazy car hair and lack of makeup, I looked pretty damn good. The dress wrapped around one shoulder and ended a few inches above my knees. The neckline was daring, but not slutty. I turned away from the mirror, and I was grateful that Drake had been thoughtful enough to carry my bag upstairs. I grabbed my straightener and cosmetics out of it. I noticed that there was a bathroom was attached to our room, and I walked inside to try to tame my hair and look somewhat presentable.

Once I was happy with my appearance, I walked downstairs to where the guys and Jade were waiting. As soon as I entered the living room, Drake had me in his arms, and he kissed me like he hadn't seen me in years. I was breathless when he finally released me.

"Get a room!" Adam yelled.

"What was that for?" I asked.

"I missed you," Drake replied.

"We were apart for all of twenty minutes."

"After being in a car with you for the past few days, it seemed longer than that."

I smiled. "You can be so freaking sweet when you want to be."

He glanced over at the guys and Jade. "Just don't tell them that. After all these years together, they still think I'm an asshole."

"We do not." Jade rolled her eyes. "You guys ready?"

"Yeah, I'm starving," Adam grumbled.

"Shut up and get your ass off my couch if you're in such a hurry," Drake said.

Adam was up and out the door before any of us could register the fact that he'd moved. I busted out laughing as the rest of us walked out the door together. Drake held me back, so the others were ahead of us.

I gave him a questioning look. "What?"

"I can't wait to rip that fucking dress off of you. You look incredible. I think I'd rather stay home and have dinner."

He raised an eyebrow suggestively, and I blushed all the way to my toes.

"Oh my God. You did not just say that!"

He grinned as he grabbed my ass and pulled me tight against him. "We'll save that for later. Let's go party."

"I thought we were having dinner?"

"We're stopping for something to eat real quick before we go to a club."

"Oh, okay." I guessed I was being thrown into L.A. life faster than I'd thought.

Chapter 13

Drake released me, and I walked over to where his car was parked. The guys and Jade were already in a car idling behind Drake's car. He waved them to go ahead, and then we got into his car and backed out of the driveway.

I started to feel nervous as we headed back to the center of L.A. I wasn't good with crowds, and I wasn't sure how I would handle being surrounded by a bunch of strangers. I hated to depend on Drake, but I definitely needed him to help me adjust to this life.

After battling the crazy Los Angeles traffic again, we pulled up in front of a sushi restaurant. As soon as we stepped out of the car, a man appeared and took Drake's key. I gave Drake a confused look, and he shook his head.

"They have valet parking almost everywhere here. You better get used to it."

"Oh, okay," I said, feeling silly.

The guys and Jade were standing by the entrance, waiting for us to join them. Once we were all inside, the hostess took us to a table in the back of the restaurant. I noticed that she had seated us far away from all the other guests. When I asked Drake about it, he explained that they'd been here before, and the staff knew who they were. They weren't being noticed a lot yet, but since their music video had been released, people had come up to them from time to time.

It was strange that all of this had already started. Once the album came out and they started touring, we wouldn't be able to just go out and do things anymore. People would know who Drake was, and they'd want a piece of him. After dealing with Kadi, I worried about stalkers now. I didn't want anything to happen to Drake, and we both knew that there were some serious nut jobs in this world.

We placed our orders, and our food was brought out shortly after. I spent the next hour catching up on what had happened with the band since I'd seen them last. They also wanted to know what had been happening in my life. It felt like I'd never been away from them. Although we weren't blood-related, these people were my family.

Right as we were getting ready to leave, my phone started ringing. I pulled it out of my purse to see that Jordan was calling.

"Hello?" I answered.

"Hey, did you make it to California yet? I haven't heard from you in a couple of days," Jordan said.

"Yeah, we made it. We're at dinner with the band right now."

"You should've called me. I was worried."

"I'm sorry. I never even thought about it. I also need to text Amber and Logan to let them know I made it."

"Yeah, you should. I'll let you go, but I wanted to make sure that you were safe."

"Thanks for thinking of me," I said.

"Always. Take care, Chloe."

"Bye, Jordan."

When I said Jordan's name, I felt Drake tense beside me, but I ignored it as I sent a text to Amber and Logan to let them know that I'd made it safely. I put my phone back into my purse and looked up to see Drake watching me closely.

"Everyone ready to go?" I asked.

"Yeah, we'll meet you guys there," Eric said.

We stood up and started walking to the door. Drake was quiet as we waited for his car to be pulled around. He was still quiet as we pulled away from the restaurant.

"What's wrong?" I asked, already knowing the answer.

"I didn't realize that you still talked to Jordan," he said quietly.

"Of course I do. He's my friend, just like Amber and Logan."

"I don't like it. I've accepted Logan in your life, but Jordan just rubs me the wrong way."

"You need to accept that I'm friends with him. It's not like I talk to him every day. We talk on the phone once or twice a week, and the last time I saw him was at Christmas."

"So, while I was being a fucking asshole out here in L.A., you were singing Christmas carols and opening presents with him?"

I sighed. "You can't be jealous of him or Logan when you're going to have women hanging all over you all the time. You have to trust me. We're starting fresh, so let's put Logan and Jordan behind us. Okay?"

"You're right. I'm being a jealous idiot. If I can accept Logan, I can accept Jordan."

"Thank you." I leaned over and kissed him on the cheek. "I promise that you're the only man I want."

"I don't know. I've seen the way you look at Adam. I'm starting to worry."

I laughed. "You're right. I can't hide my feelings anymore. I'm in love with Adam."

"I knew it!" he joked.

We pulled up to a nightclub, and just like before, a man was beside Drake by the time he got out of the car. Drake handed over his keys, and then he took my hand and walked to the door. There was a line outside the door, but the bouncer took one look at Drake and let us pass by. I saw several people glaring at us when we passed by.

"Come here often?" I joked.

"Brad thinks it's a good idea to be seen out and about in L.A. This is one of the biggest clubs in town, so we're here every weekend. I just go with it. He knows what he's doing."

"Don't the fans who recognize you come up to you?"

"Nah. The club has a VIP floor here that overlooks the main floor. People can see us, but they can't come up."

I whistled as we entered the club. "Wow."

Nothing could have prepared me for this. The bars where the band had played last summer were shacks compared to this place. The floor beneath my feet looked like it was made of glass with lights shining up through it. Above my head, hundreds of orbs in different colors were hanging every few feet. Laser lights were everywhere and in every color that I could think of. There were booths around the entire room. Each table was made of glass with lights inside of it, mimicking the floor. The seats had a band of lights across the top. I looked over to the huge dance floor. Hundreds of bodies were dancing to Icona Pop's "I Love It."

I kept my arm looped through Drake's as we walked over to a staircase. Another bouncer was standing there in front of a rope. When he saw Drake, he removed the rope and let us through without a word.

We walked up the steps to the second floor. It was a lot like the main floor, but it was a little bit fancier. When I noticed the floor was black marble, I sighed in relief. Being on the upper level, I wouldn't feel comfortable walking on glass floors, thinking that the people below us could look up and see under my dress. The booth seats were all a pristine white color with the same glass tables as below. There was a smaller dance floor on this level. My mouth dropped open as I recognized some faces from movies and music videos. Dear Lord, it was like I'd walked right into the middle of a tabloid.

Jade and the guys were already sitting at a booth next to the railing that surrounded this level of the club. We walked over and sat down with them. I took a seat against the railing that separated me from the level we'd been on moments before. I peeked through the rungs to stare down at the people dancing below us. I'd never seen so many people together like this. I was going to need some time to get used to L.A.

"What do you think?" Jade yelled from across the table.

"It's nuts. There are so many people."

She laughed. "You'll get used to it."

A waitress appeared at our table and took our drink orders. I had no clue what to order, so Drake ordered for me. A few minutes later, she appeared with all of our drinks. I was shocked at how fast she was, but Drake shrugged when I asked.

"VIP is a whole new world. They kiss your ass on just about everything."

I was silent as Drake and the band talked. I was too busy watching everyone around us. In the booth directly across from us, I saw an actor that I'd followed for years. To be sitting this close to him was unreal. I started to feel uneasy as I realized that this was going to be Drake's life from now on. How would I ever be able to fit in and feel comfortable in this world? I was so different from all of this.

"Want to dance?" Drake whispered in my ear.

I jumped. I'd been so lost in my thoughts that I had forgotten where I was. "Um, I don't think so. Have you see the people on this floor? I'll probably fall on my face in front of them."

"You'll be fine. If you start to fall, I'll catch you."

"Don't you always?" I asked.

He pulled me from the booth and led me to the floor where a few other couples were dancing. I kept my eyes on him as we started moving to the music. I was afraid to look around and see someone watching us. He smiled down at me as he pulled my body tight against his. I shivered as I felt the heat radiating off of his body. I slowly ran my hands between us and up his stomach until they were wrapped around his neck.

"You look so beautiful tonight," he whispered in my ear.

"Thank you," I said shyly.

I always felt so plain next to him, and it meant the world to me when he told me things like that. I didn't want him to ever grow bored with me.

"No thanks needed. I'm just telling you what I see." He leaned down and brushed his lips against mine. "How did I ever get so lucky?"

"I think it's the other way around," I replied.

"Not a chance. I'm the lucky one."

For the rest of the slow song, I rested my head against his chest and closed my eyes. I took deep breaths, inhaling his scent. If we were together for a thousand years, I would never get used to being with him like this.

The song ended, and a fast-paced rap song started playing.

He looked down at me and grinned. "I remember the first time I danced with you like this."

I pretended to think as we started moving with the music. "I'm not sure that I do. I mean, I've danced with so many guys."

He frowned. "Let me see if I can remind you."

He spun me around until I was facing away from him. His hips started grinding into my ass, and I gave it back to him just the same. When I felt him harden against me, heat shot between my legs. I pushed against him as I slowly slid down his body and back up. When I was standing again, he grabbed my hips and dug his fingers in as we continued to move together.

For someone who hated rap music, Drake could certainly dance to it. I forgot about everyone around us as we danced together. All that mattered was that Drake and I were together. He spun me around so that I was facing him, and then he reached around to cup my bottom.

"I want to take you right here on the dance floor," he whispered in my ear.

He ran his tongue down my neck, and I moaned in response. I dug my nails into his back as he pushed tighter against me. His body felt so good, pressed up against mine.

"Um, you guys might want to tone it down. You have an audience," Eric whispered next to us. I'd been so wrapped up in Drake that I hadn't noticed him approaching.

I pushed away from Drake and looked around. When I noticed several people staring at us, I felt my face burn from embarrassment. "Oh my God."

Drake chuckled at my embarrassment. "What's wrong?"

"Why are you laughing? We just made fools of ourselves in front of all these people."

"Who cares what they think?"

"Um, I do."

"You shouldn't. I was having fun."

I rolled my eyes. I walked back to the table and sat down. Drake had no shame. He followed me and slid in beside me.

Eric sat down across from us with a smirk on his face. "Well, at least everyone got a good show."

"Shut up, Eric," I grumbled. I laid my head down on the table.

He never tormented me, so I knew Drake and I had put on quite a show if he was.

He laughed. "Sorry, Chloe. I had to. At least I stepped in and saved you though."

Adam smacked him across the head. "Damn you! I wanted to see Chloe naked again."

My head snapped up. "Again?"

Drake shot him a glare as Jade tried to cover her laugh with a cough.

"Uh, just forget that last part," Adam mumbled.

"Oh no, you don't. Drake, when has he seen me naked?"

Drake gave me an apologetic look. "Remember when you sent me that picture last summer?"

I nodded.

"Well, Adam was standing behind me when I was looking at it, and I didn't realize it."

"Someone just shoot me and put me out of my misery!" I groaned.

"It's not a big deal. Besides, you have a smoking hot body. I couldn't look away," Adam said.

"Dude, shut up," Eric growled. "You're not helping."

"I didn't mean it as a bad thing. I would never look at you naked on purpose unless you wanted me to. If you ever do want me to, just let me know."

"I'm about two seconds away from kicking your ass. You'll never see Chloe naked again," Drake growled.

"I just meant that if you two ever wanted to take a walk on the wild side and have a threesome or something, I'm your guy."

"Shut up, Adam!" we all said in unison.

He opened his mouth to speak, but Jade put her hand over it to stop him. He rolled his eyes as he held up his hands in surrender.

Drake put his hand on my leg and started rubbing. "I'm sorry that I didn't tell you. I just didn't want you to freak out," he whispered in my ear.

Despite my embarrassment from both our dancing and Adam's confession, I shivered as Drake's breath tickled my ear. I was still turned on from our dancing, and Drake's hand on my bare leg wasn't helping the situation. Each time his hand brushed the bottom of my short dress, I swore I forgot how to breathe. He didn't notice at first as he talked with the band, but he caught on to my predicament quickly when I grabbed his hand and pushed it away.

He gave me a small smile as he put his hand back on my leg and continued to rub. Each time, he would go just a bit farther under my dress. His fingers ran along my underwear as I tried to keep my breathing even. No one else at the table seemed to notice my predicament as they continued to talk. Drake continued to be a part of the discussion as if nothing was happening.

He pushed my underwear to the side and slowly started rubbing back and forth along my clit. I tried to clamp my legs shut, but he pushed them apart with his hand and continued to stroke me softly. When he flicked my clit, I had to bite my lip to keep from moaning. I was going to kill him when we were alone.

Drake had to turn his head away to hide his smile when Jade had to ask me a question twice before I answered. I finally managed to drag my attention away long enough to answer. I almost sighed in relief when he stopped stroking me and rested his hand on the inside of my thigh. Just as my body was starting to relax, he moved his hand back and thrust two fingers inside me.

I gasped and grabbed the table. The band stopped talking and looked at me.

"You okay?" Jade asked.

"Yeah, I just had a cramp in my leg," I managed to gasp.

Out of the corner of my eye, I could see Drake grinning, but I refused to look at him. He pulled his fingers out and thrust them back in. My knuckles turned white as I gripped the table harder. The band went back to talking as Drake continued to thrust his fingers in and out of me. My breathing grew shallow as I tried to act like he wasn't about to give me an orgasm. I tried to push his hand away, but he wasn't having it. Instead, he pushed my hand away with one of his hands and started thrusting in and out faster with the other. A thin sheen of sweat broke out across my forehead as I felt myself edging closer and closer to my release. When he pulled his fingers out and flicked my clit, I came undone. I grabbed his leg and dug my nails in as I tried not to cry out. My body shook, and I rested my head against Drake's shoulder as I tried to hide what he'd done to me.

"Chloe, are you sure you're okay? You look flushed," Jade asked.

"You do. Are you not feeling well?" Drake asked, his voice full of fake concern.

"I'm not feeling that well to be honest. Maybe we should head home," I answered.

"Come on, let's get you home and into bed," Drake said.

I didn't miss his true intentions even though everyone else did.

"I'll see you guys later," I said as we stood up.

We didn't stick around to hear their response. My legs felt like jelly as I walked down the stairs and to the door. Drake kept his arm around me as we waited for his car to be pulled around. When he kissed me softly behind my ear, I shivered. I was going to kill him when we got in the car.

"That was dirty." I said the moment we got into the car.

"What?" he asked innocently.

"Don't *what* me. You shouldn't have done that in front of everyone."

"You can't tell me you didn't enjoy it." He glanced over at me. He had that shit-eating grin on his face that always melted my anger away.

"Of course I enjoyed it. That doesn't mean it was right."

"But it was fun to watch you squirm. We should do it more often."

I shook my head in annoyance, but I laughed. "I love you."

"I love you, too."

"Now," his voice turned serious, "let's get you home and into bed."

Chapter 14

The next few weeks passed in a blur. Drake and I had settled into a routine—one that I didn't like very much. Drake and the band were constantly at the label's office, trying to get things finalized for the album's release. Drake would leave early in the morning, and he wouldn't return until dinner time. He'd mentioned bringing me with him, but so far, he hadn't been able to. He promised that once things slowed down, he would.

With no school or job to keep me busy, I was bored. I hadn't found the nerve to go explore L.A. on my own. I was afraid I'd get lost or mugged. I spent most of my days reading on my Kindle or listening to music. I'd unpacked all of my things the day after I'd arrived in L.A., and I'd cleaned Drake's house the following day. Our house. I still couldn't wrap my head around the fact we had a house together. If something didn't change, I was going to get a ladder and start cleaning the windows or something equally ridiculous.

Drake and I grew closer and closer as the time passed, despite the fact that we didn't get to spend a lot of time together. Even though he wasn't around during the day, we would spend almost every evening together. Once he walked through the door, we would be glued to each other. I smiled as I remembered how he'd wanted to christen every room in the house that first week. We had done exactly that, some rooms more than once.

There was no doubt in my mind that Drake loved me and that he was doing everything in his power to stay clean. Once a week, he would go to the rehab clinic to just talk with the doctor. I was so proud of him. Despite being bored and hating his schedule, I felt like my life was finally falling into place.

After a month of solitude, Drake finally announced that I could go with him to work one day. The tour would be starting in less than a month, and they had covered all their loose ends, so things were slow for them. Dressing up a bit for the visit, I wore a short-sleeved white button-up shirt and gray dress pants with a pair of flats. I styled my hair until it was stick straight, and I put a little extra effort into my makeup. I didn't want any of Drake's coworkers to think that he could do better than me. When I told him so, Drake rolled his eyes and tried to kiss the lipstick off of my lips, but I stood my ground as I pushed him away. I didn't want to embarrass him.

I tapped my foot nervously as we drove across town to the label's building.

"Hey, calm down. They're going to love you. Even if they don't, who cares? My opinion is all that matters." Drake reached over and took my hand.

I snorted. "You always know just what to say."

"It's my gift."

When Drake parked his car in the garage underneath the label's building, I took a deep breath to prepare myself. Despite what Drake had said, I wanted these people to like me. He held my hand from the time we left his car until we walked into his manager's office. The rest of the band was already in there. Jade was relaxing on a couch next to the window while Adam and Eric were sitting on a couch on the opposite side of the room. A man was sitting behind a desk directly across from the door.

Drake practically had to drag me as he walked up to the desk. "Brad, this is my fiancée, Chloe."

Brad stood and held out his hand. "It's nice to finally meet you."

I wiped my sweaty hand on my pants before shaking his hand. "Likewise."

"Drake has told me so much about you, but he left out the part about how beautiful you are."

I blushed. "Thank you."

"So, what brings you to our office, Chloe?" Brad asked.

"I wanted to show her where I worked and introduce her to some of the people I work with. I also wanted her to meet the crew who will be on the road with us for the tour. That way, she'll know them before she's stuck on the road with them."

Brad raised an eyebrow. "I didn't realize that Chloe would be going on tour with you."

"Where I go, she goes."

Brad's phone rang, and he held up a finger as he answered. "Yes?" He was quiet as he listened to whoever was on the other end of the line. "I'll send them down now." He placed the phone back in its cradle and looked around the room at the band. "They need you guys in the studio for just a few minutes. They found a glitch on track three, and they need you to rerecord about ten seconds of the song."

"Sure. Come on, Chloe, I'll introduce you to everyone in the studio," Drake said.

"You know the rules—no one in the studio when someone is recording. She can stay in here with me, and you can come back and get her when you're done."

I felt uneasy about sitting in a room with Drake's boss by myself, but I didn't really have any other options. I smiled weakly at Drake as he nodded, and then he followed the rest of the band out the door. Trying to put some space between Brad and me, I walked over and sat down on the couch where Jade had been sitting moments before.

"So, tell me, Chloe, how long have you and Drake been together?" Brad asked.

"Um, for about a year and a half."

"That's very sweet. When do you two plan to get married?"

His questions were making me uncomfortable, but I couldn't exactly ignore him.

"We're not sure yet."

"I thought you were engaged?"

"We are."

"I'm surprised you haven't started planning a wedding already. Most women would be climbing the walls in excitement."

"We're taking our time," I answered shortly.

"I can see that. Why?"

"Sir, with all due respect, that's between Drake and me."

"Of course it is. Forgive me. I was simply trying to understand your relationship with Drake."

"I love him if that's what you're wondering."

"Of course you do. Drake is a very attractive young man with an incredible future ahead of him. I just don't want to see anything bring him down."

"What are you saying?" My body was humming with anger. Despite his warm welcome when Drake had been in the room, it was pretty obvious that this man did not like me.

"I'm just saying that Drake is at the beginning of his career. A lot of his fan base will be young women who find him attractive. I'd hate to see that disappear because he's engaged to a woman who doesn't want to marry him."

"I *do* want to marry him."

"And I'm glad to hear it. While I want Drake to be happy, I don't see how you coming on tour with him would be beneficial. The less that you're seen with him, the better. Your presence will be nothing more than a hindrance to the entire tour. The fans won't like you, and you'll take up space on the bus."

"So, you think me breaking up with him would help the overall moral of the tour?" I asked sarcastically.

"Of course not. I want Drake to be happy. In this case, I think it would be better if you kept yourself hidden. You want him to succeed, don't you?"

"That's a stupid question. You know I do."

"Then, consider staying far away from the tour. You'll do nothing but jeopardize it, and a new band doesn't need a clingy girlfriend," he glanced at me and grinned, "I mean, a clingy *fiancé* in their way."

I opened my mouth to tell him to go to hell, but then I stopped. What if he was right? During his shows over the summer, I'd seen girls glare at me thousands of times because I was sitting with him. I didn't want to destroy his career just because I didn't want him to leave me. He would never forgive me.

Brad smiled at me. "You know I'm right."

I was still speechless when the door opened, and Drake walked back in.

He stopped instantly when he saw me. "Everything okay?"

"It's fine. Chloe isn't feeling well though. Maybe you should take her home and do the studio tour another day," Brad answered.

Drake glanced at me with a worried look. "You're right. She doesn't look good. Come on, babe, let's get you home."

I stood and followed him from the office. I never said a word when we left the building or on the drive home. I was in shock. By loving Drake, I was destroying his career. I couldn't do that to him. I couldn't take his dreams away from him just because I was clingy. I wouldn't. He'd never forgive me if I took everything from him.

"Babe, what's wrong? You haven't said a word since we left Brad's office," Drake said as we walked into the house.

"Nothing. I just need to go lie down." I climbed the stairs to head into our bedroom.

The next few days passed by slowly as I battled with myself about whether or not to tell Drake what had happened in Brad's office and if I should go on tour with him. Drake continued to ask me what was bothering me, but I deflected every time. I didn't want to tell him what Brad had said to me in his office. I knew it would only make Drake angry. When he was angry, he did stupid things.

Drake finally exploded a week after my visit to the studio.

"For fuck's sake, tell me what the hell is going on!" He slammed the remote down.

We'd been sitting on the couch, watching a movie, for the past hour. I'd tried to pay attention, but it was useless. The guilt was eating me alive. I kept picturing Drake's face when the tour fell apart because of me.

"Nothing," I mumbled as I focused my eyes on the television.

"Bullshit. I've had it with this mopey Chloe. Tell me what's going on inside of that head of yours."

I looked at him with tears in my eyes. "I'm not going on tour with you."

That obviously wasn't what he'd expected me to say.

His eyebrows shot up. "Why not? Have I done something to make you angry? I swear I'm not using again."

"No, you didn't do anything. I just think it's for the best."

"There's something that you're not telling me. We had this all planned out. Now, you've suddenly changed your mind? I'm not buying it. You've been like this since I left you alone with Brad. Did he say something that upset you?"

I turned my head away from him. "No."

He ran his hands through his hair. I knew he was getting seriously aggravated when he did that.

"Why do I think you're lying? Tell me what he said."

"I'm not lying," I lied.

"Chloe…"

I sighed. "Fine. Yes, he did talk to me while you were gone."

"And?"

"He made some good points."

He growled, "Chloe, don't make me drag this out of you. Talk to me."

"You're a new band, and you're trying to build a solid fan base. A lot of those fans will be girls who like you because they want to sleep with you. It's kind of hard to increase your following when you have your clingy girlfriend on tour with you."

"Fiancée," he corrected automatically.

"Whatever. You're missing the point. You're going to lose fans because of me. I don't want to destroy your career because I can't stay away from you for a few months."

"Chloe, when it comes to music or you, I will *always* choose you. Always. I'd throw everything away as long as I knew that I had you. You're my everything."

"I won't let you throw it all away for me. It's not right."

He cupped my face, forcing me to look at him. "What else did Brad say?"

I lowered my eyes. "He doesn't understand why we aren't married yet. I'm assuming he thinks I'm using you with no intentions of marrying you. I swear that I'm not though."

"Do you want to marry me?" he asked.

My eyes snapped up to look into his. "Of course I do. I love you so much that it hurts."

"I want to marry you, too." He stood. "Stay here. I'll be back."

"Where are you going?" I asked, already knowing and dreading the answer.

"To have a little chat with Brad."

"Don't! I won't let you ruin everything for me."

"I'm not going to ruin anything. Just stay here."

With that, he grabbed his keys and walked out of the front door. I groaned as I settled back on the couch. I hadn't meant to tell him anything, but it had all slipped out. I just hoped that he didn't mess anything up because of me.

A few hours later, Drake walked back through the door. I could feel the tension rolling off of him.

"How'd it go?" I asked.

"Wonderful," he replied shortly.

"Drake? What happened?"

"I told Brad to go fuck himself."

"Drake! You didn't!"

"I did. He's a fucking asshole for even thinking what he told you, let alone saying it to your face."

214

"He's your boss! You can't do something like that because of me! You could lose everything." I was so mad at him for doing this to himself.

"I don't care. No one disrespects you. Besides, he didn't do anything except for apologize."

"Bull. There's no way he backed down. I saw the way he looked at me when he was telling me to stay away. He doesn't want your girlfriend tagging along."

He looked up at me and smiled. "I don't want my girlfriend on tour with me either."

My eyes widened in shock.

"I want my wife on tour with me."

"You'll be on tour soon. We can't plan a wedding before then!"

He ran his hands through his hair. "Fuck. As soon as we get back, we're getting married. You can make plans while we're on tour."

My pulse hammered in my ears as I thought about planning a wedding. I couldn't do something like that. I had no idea what I was doing. I would have to find a venue, find a caterer, make a guest list, pick colors, decorate, find a dress, and so many other things I couldn't even think of. I wasn't good at this kind of thing.

"Are you okay? You look like you're about to have a seizure," Drake said, his voice full of concern.

"What? Yeah. I mean, no. Oh shit, I can't plan a wedding, Drake. I just can't."

"Of course you can. It can't be that hard."

I raised an eyebrow.

"Or maybe you could ask Amber for help. She likes girlie stuff like that."

That was actually a pretty good idea. Amber was far better at being a girl than I was. I knew she wouldn't mind. She'd probably be thrilled about it.

"That might work. She'd probably do it all for me just so I don't have a panic attack."

"Is it really that big of a deal?" he asked, completely baffled by my reaction.

"Um, yes. I don't want anything big, but you're a rock star. It's kind of required."

"Says who? I don't care where or how we get married. I just want you to have my last name."

I rolled my eyes. "It's not that simple. A wedding is a huge deal. I just... I need to get my head straight and figure out what I want."

He raised an eyebrow. "You're not sure if you want to marry me?"

"No, I definitely want to marry you. I just need to figure out what I want when it comes to the wedding."

"Whatever you decide, I'm behind you all the way. I just want to be able to tell the world you're mine." He said as he kissed me softly.

I smiled. "Me, too."

Chapter 15

The album's release went off without a hitch. From the very beginning, the band and the label knew that they wouldn't break any sales records since the band was new, and they were right. Sales were slow at first, but with each passing day, they grew. Drake was constantly stressed out about it, but after he said Brad was happy with how things were going, I decided I wasn't going to worry about it. I tried to keep Drake distracted, and personally, I thought I was doing a pretty good job.

Jade had decided that we needed a girls' day, and I agreed. I loved the guys, but it was nice to get away from them. Even though Jade and I spent part of the day shopping, I still had fun. I even picked up an outfit to wear to bed for Drake. The lingerie did the trick, and he was successfully distracted for a few hours.

As the first tour date quickly approached, there was a charge in the air. I tried to stay away from it, not wanting to interfere with something that I technically wasn't part of, but it was useless. Every conversation the band had was always about the tour. When they left for their tour last summer, all of them had been relaxed and excited. This time, it was completely different. All of them felt pressured to make sure each and every show was perfect. They were too new to screw up, and everyone knew it.

Yes, they had a deal, but they still had to work their asses off to make sure their music reached every person possible.

A week before we were scheduled to leave on the tour, Drake decided he needed a break. I thought it was strange because he never quit living and breathing his music, but I didn't argue. I knew he was freaking out over this tour, and if a break was what he needed, then that was what he would get. We booked a flight to the Pittsburgh International Airport. Drake still had some stuff stored at his uncle's house, so we were going to sort through it and ship what he needed back to L.A.

I had suggested that we take the label's plane, but Drake refused. Instead, we flew first class from L.A. to Pittsburgh. Drake told me to make sure to bring sunglasses and a hat, so I could hide in case anyone spotted him. I thought he was nuts, but I didn't argue. He also told me to dress nice in case any photographers were around. I'd found a pretty white sundress while shopping with Jade, so I decided to go with that. It wasn't super dressy, but it was a lot nicer than what I normally wore.

Once we landed in Pittsburgh, we rented a car and began the almost two hour drive to Morgantown.

I was starting to get used to L.A., but it was nice to be going home. I'd once considered Morgantown to be a large city, but after my road trip with Drake and spending the last few weeks in Los Angeles, I realized just how wrong I had been. The country had a lot of amazing places, but nothing compared to the hospitality that could be found in West Virginia.

Drake had been quiet on the plane, and he continued his silence while driving to Morgantown. I tried to get him to talk, but anytime I started a conversation, he would give me one-word answers. I was seriously starting to worry about him. Drake was never quiet. I decided to give up, hoping that he would start talking on his own.

I was confused as we passed the exit we normally took to get to his house. When I asked about it, Drake cursed and apologized for not paying attention.

When we passed the rest of the Morgantown exits, I knew something wasn't right, but I couldn't put my finger on it. Then, he turned onto I-68. This would take us to his house, but it was a longer drive to get there.

When he took the exit leading to our spot by Cheat Lake, I asked, "What are you doing?"

"I thought we could stop by our old spot while we're in town."

"Oh, okay. You could have just said that, you know."

"Sorry."

I was getting pissed. Drake was purposely being short with me, and I'd done nothing wrong. I huffed as I sat back in my seat and watched the trees go by. When we entered the clearing, I knew something was going on. There were four cars parked off to the side. As many times as we'd been here, I'd never seen another car, let alone four.

"What's going on?" I demanded.

Drake smiled as he parked the car. "Get out and find out." He chuckled and stepped out of the car. "Ha! That kind of rhymed."

"Whatever you're planning, I'm going to kill you for it," I grumbled.

"I seriously doubt that."

I got out and followed him to the trail leading to the water. Once we made it down the trail to where I could see through the trees, I stopped. Amber, Logan, my cousin Danny, and the band were all standing together, waiting for us. Amber was grinning from ear to ear as she ran to me and hugged me.

"What's going on?" I asked.

"I thought you would've figured it out by now." Drake grinned at me.

"I have no clue what you guys are up to."

"You're an idiot, Chloe. You're about to get married," Amber said as she handed me a bouquet of flowers.

My mouth dropped open as I looked from Amber to Drake to where everyone else was standing. "No way."

"Way," Amber said matter-of-factly. "Come on, let's get started."

"Did you plan this by yourself?" I asked Drake.

"Nope, Amber helped. I called and told her you were freaking out about planning a wedding, so I wanted to have the most non-wedding possible. I told her about this spot, and everyone arranged to meet here. The only thing that makes this a wedding is the preacher, who is hiding behind Adam and the flowers."

My eyes filled with tears. He'd known how scared I was to plan a wedding, so he'd done it for me. "I don't even know what to say."

"All you need to say is, I do. I think you can handle that." He took my hand and led me to where everyone else was standing.

I smiled and hugged everyone, noticing that Jordan was missing. It made me sad to realize that he had to know what was going on since Danny was here, but he hadn't had the heart to show up. I regretted the fact that I'd hurt him that much.

"I'm so happy for you, Chloe," Logan whispered. He kissed my cheek and hugged me. "You deserve to be happy."

"Thank you," I whispered back, glad to know that Logan was okay with this.

The preacher had been hiding behind Adam when we arrived, but since Adam had moved to hug me, I now saw him standing by the water. He was waiting for Drake and me to walk up to him and say the words that would bind us together forever. I held Drake's hand as everyone stepped aside to allow us to walk to the preacher. My hands were sweating, and I looked over at Drake. He was no longer pretending to be quiet and stressed. Instead, he was smiling from ear to ear, looking completely relaxed. There was a happiness to him that had been missing while he was stressing over everything in L.A.

"Chloe and Drake, are you ready to begin?" the preacher asked.

"I am," Drake said.

I nodded.

"Good. Let's begin." The preacher looked around at everyone. "This is where I would normally welcome you all and ask Chloe and Drake to repeat after me, but I was informed that this is going to be the most casual wedding ever planned."

There were several chuckles from our friends behind us. This was absolutely perfect. By planning almost nothing, Drake gave me the best wedding ever. All of this was perfect for the kind of couple we were. Things between us were never planned. They just happened, and we rolled with the punches.

"Anyway, I'll let Drake and Chloe say what they need to say. Drake, care to go first?" the preacher asked.

"Sure." He turned to me. "Chloe, there's not much left to say since I've already said it all to you. Someone like you comes around once in a lifetime, and I'm lucky to have found you. From the moment I saw you when you sat down next to me in class, I knew you were mine. I've never wanted or cared about another person the way I do with you. Neither of us is perfect, but you come pretty damn close. No matter how long I live, I'll never be able to tell you that I love you enough times. Life will throw shit at us because it always does, but we'll make it through. There is nothing in this world that could tear me away from you. I love you."

I opened my mouth to speak, but he stopped me.

"Oh, and I think I was supposed to say, I do."

The preacher smiled. "Not yet. Chloe needs to make her speech first."

"My bad. Go ahead and tell everyone how much you like me, Chloe."

I laughed. "I'll try." I took a deep breath, thinking of what I wanted to say. "You were an asshole when we met. I wasn't sure if I liked you or hated you. From the first time you looked at me, you threw my entire world into chaos. Once I really got to know you, I realized you weren't an asshole at all. You're the kindest person I've ever met. No matter how bad things got, you never gave up on us even though I did. I don't know what I ever did to deserve you, but I'm grateful for every day I've spent with you and for every day that I will spend with you. I will never give up on us. I will never hurt you. We're in this until the end. I love you, Drake Allen."

"Does anyone have a reason these two should not be joined in holy matrimony?" the preacher asked. When no one spoke up, he continued, "All right then. Will Amber and Eric please bring the rings up?"

I turned to see them each pull a ring out as they walked to us. Eric gave a ring to Drake, and Amber handed me one, and then both of them walked back to where they were standing. I looked down at the ring in my hand. Once I put this on Drake's finger, he would be mine forever.

"Drake, do you take Chloe to be your lawfully wedded wife?"

"I do," he said proudly.

"Please place the ring on her finger."

He reached for my hand and slid the ring onto my finger. Tears formed in my eyes as I stared down at it. It was a simple gold ring with a row of diamonds across the top. It was perfect.

"Chloe, do you take Drake to be your lawfully wedded husband?"

"I do," I whispered.

"Please place the ring on his finger."

My vision was blurry from my tears as I reached for his hand and slipped the ring onto his finger.

"By the power vested in me by the state of West Virginia, I now pronounce you man and wife. You may kiss the bride."

The words were barely out of the preacher's mouth before Drake had me in his arms, kissing me like I'd never been kissed before. I could hear our friends shouting behind us, but their words barely registered as Drake pressed his lips against mine. The kiss went on for what felt like forever before he finally pulled away.

"I fucking love you, Chloe Allen."

"I fucking love you, too, Drake Allen."

The preacher laughed. "I'd like to introduce Mr. and Mrs. Drake Allen."

Holding each other's hands tightly, we turned to face everyone as man and wife for the first time. This was only the beginning of our new life, and I couldn't wait to experience a single moment of it. I fucking loved this man.

PART THREE

New Beginnings
Drake

Chapter  16

Seven Years Later

I took a deep breath as the stage lights dimmed. This was the last show of the tour, and I couldn't wait to get back to Chloe. She'd been on every tour with me since the beginning, but she was forced to stop traveling halfway through this tour due to the pregnancy. She was due in two weeks, and I couldn't wait to get back to her and our baby. Once I found out that I was going to be a dad, I'd decided that L.A. was no place to raise a child. I wanted him or her to grow up in a small town, like I had for most of my life.

Three months after I found out she was pregnant, I arranged for a house to be built in the clearing by Cheat Lake. It had always been our spot, and I couldn't think of a better place to raise our child. After the house was built, I had a crew come in and clear some of the trees, so we could have a big yard for our kids to play in when they were older.

We'd debated on whether or not to know the sex of the baby, and we had decided to wait. We both wanted it to be a surprise. Since we never planned anything in our lives, we didn't want to start now. It sounded stupid, but it was just the way our lives were.

I grabbed the mic from one of the crew members, and when the lights brightened, I ran onto the stage. Thousands of screaming fans were below me, all trying to push forward to get closer. I closed my eyes, soaking in their energy. While I was anxious to get home, I couldn't help but love this crowd. When it came to music, performing live was still my favorite thing to do. There was just something about it that made me feel alive. It was like I was meant to be up here.

"Are you ready to rock, Las Vegas?" I screamed into the mic.

Their answering screams were enough of an answer for me to cue Jade to start beating the hell out of her drums. Eric and Adam came in next, and then it was my turn. Our music had evolved over the years, and we'd started treading into metal instead of just rock. I loved it, but screaming into the mic for hours tended to leave my voice raw. I limited the harder vocals as much as I could though, still keeping our sound mostly rock.

I sang song after song until sweat was pouring off of me. The crowd was insane until the very end, and I hated to tell them all good-bye.

"I want to thank you guys for coming out tonight. This is our last show on the tour, and you guys have been one of the best crowds we've had. As much as I'd like to stay and hang out, I have a wife at home. She's about to have my kid, and I think I should probably get back to them."

The lights dimmed, and I walked offstage as the crowd protested. Usually, I'd give in and do an extra song or two, but not tonight. Not when a very pregnant Chloe was waiting for me. I had made it no farther than the end of the stage when I saw the crew manager running toward me.

"Drake! Chloe went into labor early! She's in the hospital now," he panted.

"Fuck!" I shouted.

I took off running. I pulled my phone from my pocket and called Brad to tell him to have our plane waiting for me at the airport. He promised that it would be ready by the time I made it there. As soon as I hung up with him, I called Amber. She'd been staying with Chloe while I was away in case she needed anything.

"Oh my God, Drake! Where are you?" Amber shouted as soon as she answered.

I reached the car and told the driver to take me straight to the airport. "On my way to the airport. What's going on?"

"Her water broke about two hours ago. I wanted to call you earlier, but she wouldn't let me. She wanted you to finish your show. She's hurting, I won't lie. The doctors say she's not fully dilated yet, but you need to hurry."

"I'm trying. Are you with her now?"

"No, they kicked me out of the room, so they could check her again. I should be able to go back into the room in just a few. I don't like leaving her alone."

"When they let you back in, tell her I'm on my way and that I love her."

"I will."

"And tell her to wait for me."

Amber laughed. "I don't think she has much say in that. Just hurry."

I hung up with Amber and then made a call to ensure I would have a car waiting for me when I arrived in Pittsburgh. I didn't want something as stupid as forgetting to arrange for a car to cause me to miss the birth of our first child.

As soon as the car stopped outside the airport, I was out and running. I knew I was taking a chance of getting mobbed by not having security with me, but I didn't care. I'd like to see anyone who could keep up with me right now. A few people glared at me as I pushed through the crowd, but no one stopped me. Once I was cleared and on the plane, I waited impatiently for takeoff. I cursed as I continued to wait. I had no idea what the pilot was doing, but he obviously didn't realize that I was in a hurry.

I was reaching to unbuckle my seat belt, so I could get up and let the pilot know my emergency, and then the plane started to move. I sighed in relief when we were finally in the air. Now, all I could do was wait.

As soon as the seat belt light went off, I was up and pacing. This was going to be the longest flight of my life. I was terrified for Chloe. She was going through this without me. I'd promised that I would be there for her, and I prayed that I would be able to keep that promise. I didn't want her to go through this without me beside her to hold her hand.

I finally collapsed back into my seat, exhausted from nerves and lack of sleep. This tour had been especially brutal, and I hadn't had a chance to sleep much. If we had more than a day between performances, I always flew home to be with Chloe. She'd decorated most of the nursery by herself since I was gone so much, but when I was home, I had spent most of the time doing the things she couldn't do. I was so damn proud when I'd put together the crib. The look on her face had been worth every curse word I'd said as I worked on it.

At some point, I fell asleep, and I woke up when the pilot announced that we were preparing to land. I fastened my seat belt and waited impatiently as the plane slowly descended from the sky. I could have cried in relief when I felt the plane touch the ground. As soon as I was cleared to leave, I ran off the plane and into the airport. I continued to run until I reached the area to pick up the key for my rental. The lady behind the desk seemed to be determined to go as slow as possible until I told her what was happening.

As soon as I located my car, I floored it. The flight from Las Vegas to Pittsburgh took almost four hours and I still had almost two hours to drive. I knew I was running out of time. The miles disappeared quickly as I flew down the interstate. Halfway to Morgantown, I realized that my phone was still shut off. I powered it on as I drove and saw I had a new voice mail. My heart was in my throat as I listened to the message Amber had left over an hour ago. It seemed that things were happening quickly, and if I didn't hurry, I wasn't going to make it. It was late, so there were few cars to avoid as I pushed my car harder. I shouted in relief when I saw the signs for my exit.

I pulled into the hospital parking lot and ran for the doors. In her message, Amber had told me what floor they were on. I opted for the stairs instead of the elevator, knowing I could run faster than it would go. When I reached the floor, I could hear Chloe screaming my name. I ran past the nurses' station and straight for Chloe's room. A nurse jumped to her feet and started shouting for me to stop, but I ignored her.

I nearly lost it when I made it to the room. Amber was beside Chloe, holding her hand, as she cried out in pain. Her hair was plastered to her forehead with sweat, and she looked exhausted. A doctor at the foot of the bed was telling her to keep pushing.

I ran to Chloe's side and grabbed her other hand. "Chloe, I'm here. I'm so sorry."

"Oh, thank God," Amber said.

Chloe looked up at me with tears in her eyes. "I can't do this. It hurts too much."

"Shh…you can do it. I'm right here with you."

"Chloe, I need you to keep pushing. We're almost there," the doctor said.

Chloe grabbed my hand and squeezed as she started pushing. I bit my lip to keep from crying out at just how hard her hand was gripping mine. I couldn't stand to see her in so much pain. Jesus, this was my worst fucking nightmare.

"That's it, Chloe. Give one more big push on the count of three. One, two, three! Push!" the doctor yelled.

Chloe screamed as she gave one final push. I couldn't breathe as I heard the single most beautiful thing I'd ever heard in my life—my baby crying.

"You did it, Chloe," the doctor said as she cut the cord and handed the baby to the nurses.

It felt like hours were passing by as I held on to Chloe's hand and waited to see my baby.

Finally, after cleaning my baby off, the nurse walked over to us with a huge smile on her face. "Are you ready to meet your son?"

"Son?" Chloe asked.

The nurse handed the baby over to her. "Yes, it's a boy."

I couldn't speak as I stared down at the little screaming bundle in my wife's arms. He was the most beautiful thing I'd ever seen. He stopped crying and snuggled into Chloe's chest as she spoke softly to him.

"You're so beautiful. I love you so much already, little guy." Chloe said as she ran her finger across his cheek.

She was crying as she looked up at me. "Come meet our son, Drake."

"Son," I whispered.

She let me take him out of her arms. He was so small. I stared at him in awe as I realized I was a dad. This baby was mine, and I would protect him with my life. I loved him and Chloe more than anything in this world.

"He's perfect." I whispered as I stared down at him. And he was. I smiled when I noticed that he had Chloe's cute little nose. With the exception of my dark hair covering his head, he was Chloe.

"Do you two have a name picked out?" the nurse asked.

Chloe smiled up at me through her tears. "We do. Meet Michael Andrew Allen."

As I stared down at my wife and son, I knew that my life was now complete. I had everything that I could ever want. Chloe and I had finally found our happily ever after.

THE END

CHLOE AND DRAKE'S STORY IS FINISHED,
BUT THE TORN SERIES ISN'T!
WATCH FOR LOGAN'S STORY,
COMING LATE 2014.

ENJOY THIS EXCERPT FROM
K.A. ROBINSON'S

SHATTERED TIES

NOW AVAILABLE AT ALL
MAJOR EBOOK RETAILERS!

COMING MARCH 2014

TWISTED TIES

BOOK TWO OF THE TIES SERIES

SHATTERED TIES

NEW YORK TIMES AND USA TODAY BESTSELLING AUTHOR
K.A. ROBINSON

PROLOGUE

Every child puts his or her parents up on a pedestal. Parents could do no wrong, and their opinions were your opinions as well.

At the tender age of six, I felt the same way. My mother, the famous supermodel, Andria Bellokavich, was my idol. I wanted to wear her clothes, make my hair look the same as hers, and share her opinions with the world.

"I can't *believe* they let that kind of riffraff in this park," my mother said as she wrinkled her nose in distaste.

I followed her gaze to see a boy around my age and his mother playing by the sandbox. "What's wrong with them, Mommy?"

"They're low-class white trash, and I don't see why they feel the need to invade *our* park."

I stared at the boy. I saw nothing low-class about him, but what did I know? My mommy knew everything, and if she said they were icky, then they must be.

"Can we make them go away?" I asked, eager to please my mommy.

"I wish, but unfortunately, this is a public park, so there's nothing I can do. I will say this—we will not be coming back here anytime soon."

I loved this park, and it made me sad that we couldn't come back. I instantly hated the boy and his mother for taking away my favorite place in the world.

"Can I go play on the slides?" I asked, not wanting to waste a minute of my time here since it would be my last.

"Of course, honey, but don't go anywhere near *them*." She sniffed as she pulled out her BlackBerry and started punching buttons.

I hated that thing. Mommy was always on it, and she never paid attention to me when she was. Daddy had one, too, but he always put it down if I wanted his attention. I didn't mind Daddy's so much.

"Thank you, Mommy!" I said as I leaped off the bench we were sitting on and ran for the slides.

I looked back once to see if Mommy was watching, so I could show her just how fast I could climb up the slide, but of course, she wasn't looking. She still had that stupid thing glued to her hand.

I sighed in defeat and slowly climbed the ladder. I was so proud of myself when I made it to the top. Not every six-year-old could climb this high without being afraid, but I could. I'd been doing it forever or at least since I was five and Mommy had started to let me run around the park on my own. She always told me that I was a big girl now and that I could take care of myself while she worked.

I sat down and pushed myself down the slide, giggling when I got to the bottom as I felt the static in my pigtails. I loved the slide. It was my favorite part of the park—after the sandbox, of course. I glanced over at the sandbox to see that the boy and his mommy had moved on to the swings.

Now's my chance! I jumped off the slide and ran as fast as I could to the sandbox. Once I made it there, I sat on the edge, so I wouldn't make Mommy mad by getting sand all over my dress. I picked up the bucket and started filling it with sand to make my very own fairy princess castle. One day, when I was all grown-up like Mommy, I would find a prince who would build me my very own castle.

"Whatcha making?" an unfamiliar voice asked.

I looked up to see the boy from earlier standing above me. I wasn't supposed to talk to him, but how could I not when he'd asked me a question?

"Making my princess castle," I replied, hoping he would lose interest after the princess part and leave me alone. If Mommy saw us talking, she would be so mad at me.

"Can I help?" he asked as he sat down right in the middle of the sandbox.

I looked around, expecting his mommy to yell at him for getting his clothes dirty, but she was just watching us and smiling as she sat on one of the slides.

"I can do it on my own," I replied shortly, hoping that he would take the hint and leave me alone.

"Don't you want to play with me?" he asked, sounding hurt.

"I'm not supposed to play with you. My mommy said so."

"Why not?"

"Because you don't belong here, and you're trash."

His eyes widened at my words, and he frowned. "I am not trash!"

"Well, my mommy says you are, and she's always right. She says you shouldn't even be allowed to play here."

"Well, your mommy is wrong. My mommy says that we are welcome here, just like everyone else."

I shrugged. "I don't care what your mommy says. My mommy is right, and you shouldn't be here. Go away."

Before he could respond, I heard my mommy calling my name.

"Emma Bellokavich Preston! Come here!"

I glared at the boy as I stood. "Now see what you've done? I'm in trouble all because of you!" I turned and ran back to my mommy. I felt a twinge of fear as I saw the angry sneer on her face.

"What did I tell you? I do not want you around people like that!"

I hung my head, ashamed that I'd disobeyed her. "I'm sorry, Mommy. I told him to go away, but he wouldn't listen."

"I don't want to hear it! If you can't listen to me, then you don't need to be here. Come on, we're going home."

I sighed as I followed her out to the parking lot where her brand-new Mercedes was parked.

All I wanted was a princess castle.

1
EMMA

Eleven Years Later

"Emma! Are you ready to go?" my mother shouted through my door.

"I'll be ready in a minute!" I shouted back as I applied eyeliner around my green eyes.

I needed complete concentration to get the smoky look that I was going for, and my mother yelling through the door wasn't helping matters. I finished applying the liner and reached for the brush sitting in front of me. I ran it through my strawberry blonde hair until it looked perfect.

Today was the first day of my junior year in high school, and I wanted to look perfect. I needed to *be* perfect. I'd managed to snag a spot on the varsity cheerleading squad my freshman year, but this was the first year that I was co-captain. I needed to set the standards for the rest of the girls on my squad. Anything less than perfection was unacceptable for the girls of Hamrick High School's State Champion Cheer Squad.

I set down the brush and grabbed my bag on the way out of my room. As I started down the stairs, my phone rang. I smiled as I listened to Ke$ha's "Die Young" playing. I had that ringtone reserved for one person and one person alone—my dad.

My parents had divorced when I was eight. My dad, Alexander Preston, traveled a lot with his rock band, Seducing Seductresses, so I rarely got to see him anymore, and I cherished every phone call that I would receive from him.

"Hi, Daddy," I said as I held my phone up to my ear.

"Hey, baby girl. Are you ready for your first day?" he asked.

"Yep. I'm getting ready to walk out the door now."

"I wish I were there to see you off," he said sadly.

I knew that he'd meant it, but like always, he was thousands of miles away from the home I shared with my mother in Santa Monica.

"Me, too. How's England treating you?"

"It's great. It's far rainier than I remembered though," he replied, sounding truly distraught about the weather.

I laughed. "You're such a dweeb, Dad."

"Did you just call your rock-god dad a *dweeb*?"

"I did. Listen, I need to go, or I'm going to be late. I'll talk to you later?"

"Of course, baby girl. Enjoy your day."

"Thanks, Daddy. I love you."

I disconnected the call and walked into our kitchen to find something quick to eat for breakfast. Our chef, Razoule, was standing by the island, holding a granola bar and smiling.

"Thanks!" I said as I grabbed the bar from his hand.

"You are very welcome, Miss Emma," he replied as he turned back to whatever he had been working on.

Razoule was one of the best chefs in the country, and my mother had managed to snag him a few years ago. After living off of his cooking for most of my life, I wasn't sure if I could handle it if he ever left us.

I walked to the front door, but just as I put my hand on the knob to open it, I heard my mother calling my name.

"Emma! Don't forget that I have a committee meeting tonight, so I won't be home until late."

"I know, Mom. You've only told me about it twenty times since last week."

"Don't use that tone with me. This is a very important meeting, and if all goes well, we will have a new and very well-known celebrity on our side."

My mother was on every committee from here to San Francisco. Since she'd walked away with a huge chunk of my dad's fortune when they divorced, she could afford not to work. Instead, she spent all her time climbing the social ladder around here, and she expected me to do the same. She only liked my friends if their parents were rich or famous or both. I loved my mom, but she was conceited and power hungry, not two things that you want to put together.

"Have a good day!" she called after me as I opened the door and walked out into the bright sunlight.

I slipped my sunglasses over my eyes and smiled as I walked to my car. I loved California. The weather was perfect, the beach was just a short drive away, and the entire place was beautiful. I'd traveled some with my dad over the years, but no place could ever come close to California.

I attended a private school, Hamrick High School, with most of Santa Monica's finest. Rather, I attended it with the demon spawn of Santa Monica's finest. When mommy and daddy were gone most of the time and they supplied you with endless amounts of cash, the perfectness that surrounded our school and the students attending all but disappeared. Underneath were wild parties, drunken fights, and more than one crashed sports car. Lucky for me, I was at the heart of it all.

I played the perfect daughter and the perfect student by day, but when the parents disappeared and the alcohol flowed, I liked to party with the best of them. Chalk it up to my mommy and daddy issues, but I used the parties as an escape from reality. After all, who is really perfect when it comes right down to it?

My school was less than ten minutes from my house, and I arrived before I'd even managed to finish my granola bar. I parked my brand-new Mercedes-Benz next to my best friend, Lucy's, Jaguar and stepped out. Students were everywhere. Most were standing by their cars while others, the more responsible ones, were walking up the steps to the school.

I caught sight of Lucy's dark brown hair in a crowd of people next to the stairs. I snuck quietly over and launched myself onto her back. Her squeals of terror had everyone laughing as she tried to throw me off. I finally gave up and released her after I thought she'd suffered enough.

She turned to glare at me. "That was so not cool, Emma!"

"It might not have been cool, but it was funny," I said as I giggled.

She rolled her eyes as she linked her arm through mine, and we started walking up the steps to the school.

"Lookin' good, Emma," Todd Bex said as he walked past us.

I sighed dreamily as I watched him walk by. Todd was a senior and the captain of the football team. Add in his good looks and charm, and he was the most sought-after guy in our school. I rarely wasted my time on boys, but he wasn't a boy. He was a man. He kept his dark hair cut short most of the time. His eyes were a beautiful baby blue, and that, coupled with a strong jawline and full lips, made every girl turn to mush at his feet. The fact that he had talked to me, a lowly junior, sent thrills through my body. Maybe this would be the year that someone finally tamed him, and that someone could be me.

"Wipe the drool off your face," Lucy teased.

I stuck my tongue out at her. "Shut up."

She opened her mouth to reply, but she was cut off when we heard a loud backfire coming from the parking lot. Both of us turned to see a beat-up Jeep pulling into the lot and parking beside my car.

I raised my eyebrows in disbelief. *Who on earth is driving something like that around here? And why do they feel the need to park next to me?*

"Who is that?" I asked as we watched a guy climb out of the Jeep and walk toward us.

"I have no idea, but I wouldn't mind finding out," Lucy replied as she stared at the new arrival with lust-filled eyes.

I squinted, trying to see him as he walked toward us. He looked vaguely familiar, but I couldn't place him. Lucy squeezed my arm as he looked up and noticed us staring. I thought my arm was actually going to fall off when he approached us and stopped directly in front of me.

"Hi. I was wondering if you could tell me where the office is," he said politely.

Now that I could see him up close, I understood Lucy's excitement. *Wow. Just wow.* I had been ogling Todd not two seconds before, but I had to admit that this guy was far better than Todd. His hair was a shaggy mess of blond curls, and his eyes were the brightest emerald green that I had ever seen. His upper lip was a bit thin, but his bottom was full and just begging to be kissed. He was wearing a fitted polo shirt, and it stretched to its limit every time he moved due to the muscles that it was concealing. Several tattoos covered his arms, and they were a total contradiction to how he was dressed. This boy looked like a fallen angel and a surfer boy all rolled into one, and I wanted to wrap myself around him.

I blushed as I pictured us together, both wearing nothing but a smile. *Dear Lord, what has gotten into me?* Yes, I was a partier, but I'd never been in *that* situation before. Virgins didn't imagine total strangers naked, yet here I was, picturing him naked.

"I'm Lucy," she said as she held out her hand for him to shake.

He took it and smiled. "I'm Jesse. It's nice to meet you, Lucy."

She gave him her brightest smile as I stood frozen.

"And this is Emma," Lucy introduced me.

He held out his hand to me, and mine rose on its own to meet his. When our hands touched, I felt like I'd been shocked, and I pulled back quickly.

"It's nice to meet both of you," he said politely.

"Uh, yeah. You, too," I said lamely. I knew Lucy was going to have a field day with this later.

"Anyway, can you point me in the direction of the office?" he asked again.

"Oh, right. Of course." I turned and pointed to the doors where several students were walking through to go to their first class. "Just go through those doors and make a left. It's right down the hall."

He smiled. "Thanks so much for your help."

I watched as he walked around us and made his way through the doors.

253

"Holy shit. I think I'm in love," Lucy groaned as she stared at the empty spot where he'd just been standing.

"Wow," was all I could manage to get out. My brain wasn't functioning at the moment.

"Yeah, wow. I don't think I've ever seen you freeze up like that," she teased.

"I just…wow. I don't know what happened."

"I think we both have it bad," she said as we walked up the rest of the steps and headed into our school.

I remembered him pulling in with his piece of crap car. "I wonder who he is. He has to be a new student since I've never seen him before, but I don't see how since he drove up in that thing."

"Maybe he's one of the scholarship kids," she suggested.

"Scholarship kids?" I asked stupidly.

"Do you ever pay attention? Coach Sanchez was just talking about it the other day at practice. I guess the school awarded scholarships this year to two or three kids from across town. They normally attend the public school over there."

"Oh," I said.

"Yeah, oh. That has to be it. I would have remembered seeing that guy before now. He's not exactly someone you can forget."

"So, if he went to the public school, he must be poor," I said, sounding disappointed. There was no way I would ever be able to get to know him. My mother wouldn't allow it.

"Do you realize how snobby you just sounded? I swear to God your mother's voice just came out of your mouth."

I rolled my eyes. "You know what I mean. My mom would never let me associate with someone like him."

"Because he isn't rich?" Lucy asked sarcastically.

"Because he isn't rich."

"Your mom is a bitch."

"And so is yours. They both run in the same circles, you know."

ACKNOWLEDGMENTS

To me, this is the hardest part of a book to write. There are so many people who have helped me, and I know I will miss a few.

To my husband—Without you, I would never have finished any of my books. You're my rock.

To my parents—You listen to me and help me with everything I need. I wouldn't be who I am today without you.

To my blogger friends—Gah! I can't say thanks enough times to all of you. You're not *just* bloggers to me. You're my friends. Without you, no one would even know who K.A. Robinson is. No one would know who Drake is. (That would be a damn shame right there, wouldn't it?) Your support means so much to me.

To my "real-life" friends—Thank you for dealing with my constant absence. I know it's hard to get a hold of me. I get so into writing that I forget to live sometimes. You're always there to drag me back to reality. I love you!

To my author friends: Tabatha, Katelynn, Sophie, Tijan, and several others I know I'm forgetting—I love you. Seriously. You guys keep me calm, help me when I need it, and remind me to eat. I feel so blessed to call you my friends.

To my readers—Your response to Chloe and Drake has been overwhelming. I *never* imagined that so many of you would care about these two characters the way you do. You guys continue to rock my world on a daily basis. I love you all to pieces.

To Letitia—You make the best covers. Ever. Thank you!

To Jovana—You deserve a medal for dealing with my crazy self and for reading the unedited mess of a book that I send to you. You rock!

ABOUT THE AUTHOR

K.A. Robinson is twenty-three years old and lives in a small town in West Virginia with her toddler son and husband. She is the *New York Times* and *USA Today* Bestselling Author of The Torn Series. When she's not writing, she loves to read, usually something with zombies in it. She is also addicted to coffee, mainly Starbucks and Caribou Coffee.

Her latest novel, *Shattered Ties*, was released on November 12, 2013.

Facebook: www.facebook.com/karobinson13
Twitter: @karobinsonautho
Blog: www.authorkarobinson.blogspot.com

CPSIA information can be obtained at www.ICGtesting.com
Printed in the USA
LVOW10s1022210815

451046LV00004B/114/P